Trading heels for hiking boots.

Rock Bottom Romance

DIANE HOLIDAY

CITY OWL
PRESS

ROCK BOTTOM ROMANCE

CITY OWL PRESS
www.cityowlpress.com

Cover Design by MiblArt. All stock photos licensed appropriately.

Edited by Mary Cain.

For information on subsidiary rights, please contact the publisher at info@cityowlpress.com.

Print Edition ISBN: 978-1-64898-429-7

Digital Edition ISBN: 978-1-64898-430-3

Printed in the United States of America

This book is dedicated to all the people who are devoted to helping animals.

Praise for Diane Holiday

"Holiday delivers another fast-paced read with heart and humor in *Rock Bottom Romance*." — *USA Today Bestselling Author of Historical Romance, Renee Ann Miller*

"Full of moments that will make you smile. *Rock Bottom Romance* is a feel-good novel that will have you rooting for the hero and heroine right from the moment they meet." — *Young Adult Romance Author, Miguella Twosias*

"This was an amusing read with relatable characters I couldn't stop rooting for." — *Historical Fiction Author, KA Nelson*

"*Love Uncovered* blends the tension of a high-stakes corruption case with the charm of a well-realized small-town setting to create a fun, fast-paced story." — *Publisher's Weekly*

"A fast-moving, exciting novel. The main characters are the perfect combination of charming and complex. This contemporary romance delivers electrifying heat between characters with a sprinkle of humor." — *InD'tale, Tina Donovan*

"Diane Holiday's debut, *Love in Hiding*, kept me hooked from the first page to the last." — *USA Today Bestselling Author of Historical Romance, Renee Ann Miller*

"A strong heroine, sexy hero and downright scream-worthy villains —a page-turner with spunky dialogue and suspense that kept me up way past my bedtime because I just couldn't put it down." — *Contemporary Romance Author and Golden Heart® Award Finalist, Christina Hovland*

"*Love in Hiding* combines the laid-back atmosphere of country life with the suspense angle of a crazed stalker beautifully. Great characterization, perfect pacing and witty dialogue top off this exceptional read." — *Jessie Gussman, author of Sweet Water Ranch*

"Solid storytelling featuring a classic hero and a daring heroine." — *New Adult Author and Golden Heart® Award Winner, C.R. Grissom*

"A man scarred by guilt, a feisty woman, and a villain who is totally evil make Diane Holiday's *Love Uncovered* a fast-paced read that sizzles with both romance and suspense." — *USA Today Bestselling Author of Historical Romance, Renee Ann Miller*

"Diane Holiday's well-crafted romantic suspense stories keep readers turning the pages, ready for the next twist! I always look forward to her books." — *Contemporary Romance Author and Golden Heart® Award Finalist, Christina Hovland*

"Holiday writes romantic suspense with just the right balance of heart and heart-pounding action." — *USA Today Bestselling Author, Dylann Crush*

"*Love on the Line* is an excellent story in the vein of time-honored romance--suspense, love, and characters who keep you turning the pages." — *Contemporary Romance Author and Golden Heart® Award Finalist, Christina Hovland*

"Two people looking for the opposite things in life find out they might be a perfect match. But danger lurks when they fall under the spotlight of a madman. Love on the Line is a suspenseful read." — *USA Today Bestselling Author of Historical Romance, Renee Ann Miller*

"Love on the Line delivers a romantic suspense with strong characters you'll remember long after you read the last page." — *New Adult Author and Golden Heart® Award Winner, C.R. Grissom*

"Well-plotted, beautifully written and completely engrossing, Love on the Line is absolutely the best romantic suspense I've read this year." — *Jessie Gussman, author of Sweet Water Ranch*

"Both intense and hot, Love on the Line keeps readers flipping the pages! Sexy romance and thrilling suspense--there's nothing else one could ask for!" — *Young Adult Romance Author, Miguella Twosias*

"What begins as a cruel bet...soon becomes a terrifying, life-threatening game of cat and mouse. The chemistry between Holiday's protagonists is intense and believable." — *Publisher's Weekly*

Also by Diane Holiday

LOVE BEYOND DANGER SERIES

Love in Hiding

Love Uncovered

Love on the Line

Chapter One

Crystal Lovechild would rather be caught without makeup by paparazzi than scout another wretched location for a campground-set reality show. From the passenger seat of a dented SUV, she tugged at the seatbelt, chafing her neck. She checked her fresh manicure and let out a breath. All good. The tips and polish would have to last throughout filming. How she longed for the days when she arrived at a gig in a chauffeured limo with her own hair, makeup, and wardrobe team.

"You gotta be shitting me. More wild turkeys?" Sydney, her field producer, leaned on the horn. She blew her purple-streaked bangs up and slapped the steering wheel. The flock jerked, separated, and trotted off the road.

"Are we almost there?" Crystal gazed out the window. They sure as hell weren't in Hollywood anymore. Cows grazed behind miles of fences. This spot in the Midlands of South Carolina took the prize for the most remote of the four locations they'd scouted and showed the least promise. Nothing but farms, fruit stands, and blood-thirsty mosquitos. She shuddered and scratched her now itchy arm.

"We're close." Sydney's pierced lips twisted. "Not exactly what you're used to, is it?"

"I'll be fine." Crystal hoped.

Sydney was a real pain in the ass with a chip on her shoulder a mile high, knowing the star of the show would be a fallen celebrity. From the moment they'd met, the woman had doled out one back-handed insult after another. People loved to see a famous person out of their element. The concept of a celebrity learning to rough it camping had thrilled test audiences, but Sydney's production company couldn't afford an A-list actor. She'd made sure Crystal knew she'd been their *last* choice in the low-budget production.

Since subletting her Hollywood penthouse wasn't enough to put a dent in Crystal's bills, it was the reality show or wait tables. So not happening. She cringed at the mere thought.

She glanced at her silent phone, and a pit formed in her stomach. No texts, messages, or calls, aside from Jenna, Crystal's long-time friend, the one person who hadn't ghosted her.

Sydney slowed for yet another turn in the road. "I hope you like hot dogs and beans because there's no caviar on the island."

"It's two months. I'll survive." A bead of sweat trickled down Crystal's back. Her agent had made it clear it was this gig or nothing. Crystal needed a spark to get people talking about her again, and any screen time counted. Besides, how hard could camping be?

At last, they reached the gate. A sign that read "Stone Island Park" marked the entrance. Sydney stopped at the admissions booth and opened the window.

Hot humid air rushed in. The temperature topped ninety and it was only the first week of June.

A short, stout woman, wearing a khaki safari shirt and shorts, stepped out of the booth.

Sydney handed her a business card. "We're with the production company for *Celebrity Trials.*"

"Yeah, I heard y'all were coming to check out the island. You're gonna love it." The park attendant bent and peered at Crystal's glittery halter tank, miniskirt, and stilettos. Her lips twitched and her eyebrows knitted. "That's...quite the outfit."

"Thank you." Crystal's chest inflated and rose like a hot-air balloon. She'd glammed up for scouting the sites. In the end, she might decide she didn't want them to use any of the footage, but if she did, she'd give her fans a glimpse of the star they knew and loved. Couldn't hurt to start off with some confidence, and it might be a while before she could dress in her fashion line of clothes again.

The attendant straightened, scratched her head, and checked the road behind them. "I expected a row of cars. You know, full of bodyguards and reporters."

"I don't think she has to worry about paparazzi anymore." Sydney smirked.

Crystal's blood heated. The truth stung. Even if she had the money to pay for a bodyguard, she wouldn't need one. She'd lost mega followers and subscribers on social media. No one tried to sneak candid shots anymore.

The park attendant grabbed a pamphlet from the booth and handed it to Sydney with a big smile. "Here's a map. Feel free to stop back and ask any questions. We're excited for y'all to be here."

Sydney thanked the woman and pulled forward. "Trevor is meeting us at the campsite for the opening shoot. I hope the cameras are all set up because I need him to capture your arrival. If not, I'll have to help him again like the last time when he was running behind."

"Don't look at me," Crystal replied. "I only know one side of the lens."

"I wasn't holding my breath, hoping for your assistance." Sydney's cheeks puffed.

They crossed a long bridge over the lake with water rippling on both sides. Random small boats peppered the shoreline as fishermen cast near the rocks. What fish was worth baking in the sun and bouncing around in the water all day? No thanks. Plated and served was more Crystal's style.

She gazed at the woods on either side of the single-lane road beyond the bridge and shook her head. "Why don't we save us all some time and turn around? This is too remote."

"You haven't even seen the camp yet."

"I've seen enough." Crystal dusted her hands of the place. "Go back. We're done here."

Sydney hit the brakes and turned to Crystal, her face bright red. "I've had it with you. I busted my ass for four years to work my way up to producer, and this is my big chance. I'm not about to let some washed-up child star living off her past celebrity status blow it. The contract says the company picks the site, not you. Got it?"

Crystal's throat constricted. Damn. She hadn't read the contract. That's why she had an agent, who should have told her about the stipulation.

She huffed. "Fine. Let's get it over with then."

Sydney pulled into a shady parking spot on a campsite loop. "Looks like Trevor is ready for us."

He stood by a cement slab surrounded by woods with a trail that led to the lake. Just like at the other locations, people pitched tents on concrete here. Crystal's hips and elbows ached at the thought. She'd hoped for a more comfortable arrangement. Maybe she'd buy a foam pad like the one she had for her bed. The thicker, the better. As soon as she had money for one, she'd order it.

With her well-practiced, red-carpet smile pasted on, she opened the car door. She pushed out of the SUV, making sure to pause as her heels hit the ground for the best toned-legs shot. Not that it mattered, because she had no intention of working on this island.

For now, she'd play along.

She crinkled her nose and shrugged. "I think my viewers will be bored with this remote place. The other sites had way more campers and action."

The roar of an engine cut through the silence. She spun around as some sort of jeep or four-wheeler thingy came to a halt next to them.

A mountain of a man jumped off the vehicle wearing camo pants and an olive T-shirt stretched to the max over his broad shoulders. The fabric clung to the rippled muscles of his stomach. He radiated pure strength with corded veins in his neck and not an ounce of fat on him. She judged him to be about her age, late twenties.

He had a buzz cut and a couple of days of stubble on a chiseled face. His prominent, strong jawline clenched as he strode toward them. This guy moved with purpose and power, like a big black bear on its hind legs defending his territory.

Crystal swallowed and tried to ignore the fluttering under her ribs. The unfamiliar feeling caught her off guard. Sure, she'd worked with macho types in the movies, but Hollywood used special effects and cosmetics to make them appear larger than life.

Aviator glasses hid his eyes, yet she sensed anger emanating from him. What was his problem?

Sydney made a keep-the-cameras-rolling hand gesture to Trevor.

Great. Sydney and Trevor couldn't be on film, so it was up to Crystal to deal with the man.

He stopped in front of her, planting his feet in a wide stance. "I'm Zach Stone. Obviously, you are the celebrity whatever crew." The sides of his mouth turned down. "I run this campground."

Not the most welcoming hello. And either he didn't care enough to know the name of the production company, or he'd dissed it on purpose. She smoothed back her hair and shrugged. "Doesn't look like much to manage. A bunch of woods and tents. What's the worst problem? Sunburn?"

He snorted and his chest expanded.

She tore her gaze from his pecs to his face, and her own reflected in his mirrored sunglasses. Her cheeks heated, and they turned pink before her eyes. What the hell? She didn't blush. Then again, she'd never been this close to someone so...daunting.

"What's this getup?" He waved a hand from her head to her feet. "You plan to camp in that?"

Her skin prickled. Getup? He should be thrilled she'd even considered wearing one of her designer outfits to his Podunk grounds. From the corner of her eye, she noted Trevor had moved closer, zooming in on them.

"I'll have you know this is the latest in my line." She smoothed a hand down her side and squared her shoulders. "It's so popular I can't even keep up with the orders." If only that were true.

Zach's head dipped and snapped back up. Was he checking her out?

"Cut." Trevor lowered the camera. "This thing's on the fritz again. I have to get the other one from the villa."

"That's fine. I need more coffee anyway." Sydney checked her watch. "We'll grab some at the general store and meet again in half an hour?"

Trevor nodded.

"I'll make sure I'm here," Zach said.

Crystal raised her chin. "We don't need you to be. Why don't you do whatever you do while we check out the place?"

"Keeping people like you from getting hurt while stomping around my territory unsupervised *is* what I do. I'll be back."

Crystal glared at him as he stalked to his vehicle. Her face burned. The guy had a bad attitude and a load of arrogance to go with it.

Just another reason to make sure they chose a different location.

Like hell he'd have the last word. She had a thing or two to say to him before she left him in the dust.

Chapter Two

Zach stretched out the six-foot-long snakeskin he'd found in the brush on the island.

Impressive.

Seeing that should send the reality show crew packing. If not, he had other weapons in his arsenal. He didn't get off on scaring people, but that ditz needed a wake-up call. Who showed up in high heels and a miniskirt to a campsite?

Unreal.

His phone rang with Levi's ringtone. His younger brother ran the marina.

"What's up?" Zach asked.

"Brody said Crystal was coming today. Have you seen her?"

He puffed out a breath and shook his head. His older brother, Brody, oversaw the island operations and managed the finances. He and Levi had outvoted Zach on the decision to let the producers consider the campgrounds to film *Celebrity Trials*. Hell, Levi had drooled at the prospect, saying it would bring in business.

"I've seen her all right."

"Is she as hot in person as she looks in the media?"

An image of Crystal popped into his head. She'd been tinier than he'd expected, but with curves in all the right places. He hadn't missed her toned arms and legs on full display. His blood warmed. Even her perky nose and the cute way the end turned up had caught his attention. Not to mention her shiny blond hair, gleaming in the sun.

"Zach, you there?"

"Yeah." What was wrong with him? He didn't like or want Crystal around.

"Yeah, as in she's hot?"

"Don't you have work to do?" He swatted a mosquito.

"You know what they say, all work and no play—"

"This isn't funny, Levi. I never should have agreed to majority rules when it comes to the business." Zach stepped over a log and stomped toward the lake. "What do you and Brody care if some spoiled socialite turns my campsite into a carnival? I have no idea why she'd even want to be in a show that's going to make her look like a fool. You want this washed-up celebrity here so badly, have her learn to fish or something and stay the hell out of my territory."

"Hey, I'd go for that. Lighten up, bro. You take things too seriously. She's—"

"I don't have time for this. Gotta go." He hung up, his blood pulsing in his veins. Levi's infatuation with Crystal ate at him, which pissed him off even more.

Not that he followed any celebrities, but he didn't live under a rock and had seen Crystal's face splashed across the tabloids. She lived the high life, surrounded by materialistic people. No thanks. He knew the type and had nothing in common with them. Crystal and her posse could stay in Hollywood where they belonged.

He stopped and glanced around the calm woods. His solace. His place of respite. His controlled, safe, and secure space.

Brody and Levi had no idea what Zach had experienced overseas. He kept that buried deep inside. They wouldn't understand his trauma and might question his ability to run the camp. That's the last thing he needed, especially with his mother banking on them to keep the family business alive.

The oak leaves rustled in the breeze. High in the sky, an osprey floated in the wind, dipping one wing then the other as it glided in lazy circles. A squirrel scampered across the grass, picked up a nut, and nibbled the top. Zach took in a deep breath, and his shoulders loosened.

He walked to the lake's edge. After tossing off his shoes, he waded in, scooped a handful of the fresh water, and splashed his face. The cool liquid washed away some of the angst from his perpetual memories.

A fishing boat coasted to the shoreline. In the quiet cove, the repetitive whip of a cast and reel spinning echoed across the smooth water.

Click.

Whirr.

Plunk.

Zach dug his feet into the soft, sandy lake bottom and breathed in the pine-scented air. No way he'd let some production company light up his camp, scare the wildlife, and overrun his bunker. All the activity might trigger him, and he couldn't risk an episode in front of everyone. He knew firsthand how people reacted to his incidents. This was his safe haven, and he'd keep it that way.

He needed a strategic plan that might involve more than a snakeskin.

When he came up with one, he smirked. By the time he got done, *Celebrity Trials* would want nothing to do with Stone Island Park.

Chapter Three

Crystal's back stiffened as Zach marched toward them, carrying a stack of papers. Same as last time, he moved with purpose, his mouth set in a grim line.

Sydney stood to the side, out of camera range while Trevor filmed.

Zach stopped in front of Crystal, and she crossed her arms. She had a few words for him. "Do you roll out of bed an angry elf or is this performance just for our benefit?"

"You're the so-called actress. You tell me."

So-called? Now he was mocking her. She dug her nails into her elbows. "I'll have you know—"

"Save your breath. I don't have time for this." He handed her the pile of papers. "Before you make a decision about using this location, you'll need to read all the rules and precautions for camping. Especially the section on bears."

"Bears?" She blinked. Her legs quivered as she peered into the forest. At night a dark animal would be hard to see.

Zach shrugged. "That seems to be people's biggest fear. Always good to know what to do in an encounter."

She'd swear she was having one right now, with him. "Grizzly." The pile of papers he'd handed her could fill a five-inch binder. Her eyes would cross before she got halfway through. Besides, they'd be picking a different location. She thrust the stack back at him. "I'm not much of a reader."

"What does that mean?" His eyebrow hitched above the dreaded aviators.

"I learn more from videos and chatting with people than slogging through documents. Social media, YouTube, Facebook, that kind of thing."

Zach placed his hands on his hips, refusing to take back the paperwork. "You won't find *my* rules there."

Part of a tattoo peeked out from under his sleeve. Numbers of some sort, maybe a date? Below the ink was a jagged scar about three inches long on his bulging biceps. The wound only added to his all-male, rugged vibe. Her mouth went dry and that flutter under her ribs returned.

She'd never had this reaction to anyone. Something about him was different. He didn't fit the mold of a sculpted gym rat. He had a rawness about him, like he could wrestle an alligator and win. If he'd lose the bossiness, she might appreciate he wasn't trying to impress or fawn over her.

He waved at her clothing. "Speaking of safety, this outfit won't work unless you cover yourself in DEET. Spray your entire body and that still might not keep you from getting bit."

"No way. I don't put chemicals on my skin."

He shook his head. "That's what the last camper said before she got a brown recluse spider bite and spent a week in the hospital."

Oh no. Spiders? Her skin crawled. She brushed her legs down and stomped her feet.

"Can't hurt to do that, but it's better to wear the right clothes. He tapped his boot on the ground. "By the way, I'd suggest you stand on the concrete. Your pedicured toes are perfect bait for fire ants."

Crystal scanned the dirt around her feet. Sure enough, ants crawled in the soil. Wasting no time, she stepped onto the slab. "Is that what those are?"

"Nope. Fire ants are small and red. They form big mounds of dirt—like that." He nodded to an orange clay cone the size of a basketball. "If you happen to step on one, they race out and can cover your body in no time. When the queen gives a pheromone signal, they all bite at once."

Holy crap, she hadn't signed up for this shit. Her pulse beat faster and more sweat dripped down her back. Biting her lip, she surveyed the ground surrounding the cement. With a gasp, she pointed to the foot of a nearby tree. "Oh my God. Is that a... a...snake?"

Zach squinted. "I'll be damned."

"So yes?" She took a step back.

He strode to the tree and picked up a snakeskin, stretching it out to at least six feet long. "This looks like a recent shed. Magnificent."

Crystal sucked in a sharp breath, and her stomach heaved. "That's not the word I'd use."

"Why not? It's part of nature. Isn't this why you're here? To take in the whole experience?" He let go of one end of the skin and it swung from side to side in the breeze.

That snake had to be freaking huge. Sydney made a strangled laughing sound, and Crystal yelled at her, "This is *not* funny."

The smirk remained on Sydney's face, and Trevor kept filming.

Grizzly continued to examine the skin. "Surprised to see a water moccasin up here. They usually stay by the lake. She must have a nest nearby."

"You mean she's still around?" Crystal clutched the stack of papers to her chest.

"Well, she isn't in *this* anymore. She'll be easier to see though, since she's bigger now." He carried the skin to his vehicle and tossed it in the back. "Up here, we usually find copperheads and rattlesnakes, not moccs."

Crystal's insides shook, and she shuddered. No one had said anything about venomous snakes. They could sneak inside her tent at night. And never mind the bears, fire ants, and spiders. "What are you going to do with that thing?"

"Throw it in the lake for the alligator turtles to eat."

"There aren't any alligators around here. I looked it up before we came." She'd at least checked that out.

"I said alligator *turtles*. You'll want to steer clear of them too." He folded two fingers down. "One chomp and you can lose a couple of digits."

He had to be messing with her. "There's no such thing."

"Don't believe me? Check it out online."

She grabbed her phone and typed in a search. Images appeared of prehistoric-looking turtles with fang-like, sharp beaks. Good God. They resembled monsters. The phone shook in her hand as blood drained from her limbs. "These are here? In the lake?"

"Yeah, but they come up on the land too." He adjusted his aviators and rocked back on his heels. "You don't seem very prepared. Did you do any research before you showed up in these ridiculous clothes with no idea how to survive the elements?"

Her temper lit at his cocky, condescending attitude. "How dare you question me and make fun of my fashion statement while you hide behind those bug-eyed glasses and dole out insults? You should be grateful I'm even here. My show could put this no-name-nothing island on the map."

"Hide?" Zach's nostrils flared. "No-named island?" He took a deep breath. When he raised his sunglasses, the full force of his sparkling-green, emerald eyes bored into hers.

Wow.

Beautiful, yet haunting. A zip of energy traveled up her spine, causing goosebumps to form on her arms. Something flashed in his eyes when he'd looked at her without the glasses. A quick spark, like he'd felt the energy too, but she could have been wrong.

Through gritted teeth, he said, "This place has a family name: Stone Island Park. And we don't need you to put us on any map."

He lowered the sunglasses, cutting her off again.

Okay, maybe she'd gone too far, but damn it, he'd pushed her buttons. And that not fawning over her thing? Not so endearing now. Some fawning would be nice.

They stood at arm's length, neither one budging.

His phone buzzed, and he tilted his shades up to check the message. Of course, that deserved his full attention, not her. Screw him. She couldn't wait to tell Jenna about this jerk.

"Gotta go. There's a black widow on a porch in the villas."

A pang of fear gripped Crystal's heart. A black widow? Those were deadly too. Enough already. This place was a death trap.

As he climbed into his vehicle, she hurried to the passenger side and threw the pile of papers on the seat. "We won't be needing these."

Crystal yelled to Sydney, "Pack it up. No freaking way we're filming here."

Chapter Four

Z ach wiped the sweat off his brow as he drove his side-by-side to the island general store. Crisis averted. Crystal and her crew would never step foot on his campgrounds again. They'd hightailed it out of there faster than spooked deer.

He'd thrown as much as possible at her. To her credit though, she'd stood toe to toe with him and hadn't backed down. Sure, she'd fled from the place, but not from *him*. When he'd glared into her sapphire eyes, he'd swear he glimpsed something deep. Not what he'd expected. Clear, honest, and almost vulnerable for the briefest of seconds.

He'd slapped his shades back down because it was bullshit. She spent her life in front of a camera and knew how to act. Nothing could be real about her, including that ludicrous last name, Lovechild.

Enough.

Done, gone, and for the better.

He parked next to the store, climbed the steps to the park office, and entered. Stacks of folders covered the rustic desk their dad had crafted from a fallen tree. Dust particles shimmered in the sunlight, streaming through the open window, and the scent of pine filled the room. Brody sat behind the desk, staring down at paperwork.

"Why'd you call a meeting? I have work to do." Zach took a seat across from him.

Brody glanced up and back to a folder. "Let's wait for Levi so I don't have to repeat everything."

Great. If his younger brother had hot women on his pontoon trip, no telling when he'd return.

Zach ran his campsites and cabins on military time with everything on a schedule, like in the army. A concept Levi would never understand. "Tomorrow is turn-over day, and I'm busy. Why don't you text me when he gets here?"

"Is this where the party is?" Levi called from the doorway, sporting a Hawaiian shirt and swim shorts, his go-to uniform for boat tours. With a tanned body, and long, wavy blond hair, his California surfer look drove all the women crazy. The total opposite of dark-haired Zach and Brody.

"You're late." Brody frowned.

"Sue me. I was getting a phone number." Levi grinned and took a long drink from a bottle of ice tea. "Need to cool down. Things were hot out there, if you get my drift."

Zach tapped his foot and gestured to Brody. "Can we get on with the meeting?"

Brody straightened. "I went over the books again, and we're in trouble."

"You worry too much." Levi waved a dismissive hand. "Every year things work out."

"Not this time. I found out our insurance company won't cover the collapsed ceiling and water damage to the Great Room because of an exclusion clause in the policy. I did the math. We need that building to keep us afloat with all the events and parties we have booked. Even if we're at full capacity all season long, we won't make enough money and could lose this place." Brody opened the folder and pulled out some papers.

Zach's gaze went to a picture on the wall of his father in a golf cart, a huge smile on his face. He'd loved riding through the park on that thing. Zach's heart squeezed. After his military career, his dad had started with the campgrounds and expanded to include the marina and villas. This place had meant everything to him. Zach held a thumb up. "What if we raise the prices?"

"We can't charge enough to cover the repairs needed and earn the capital to expand the marina to full-service. People won't pay it. This is a small island on a lake, not a waterfront resort on the Caribbean," Brody said.

"Maybe we can take out a loan?" Zach hated the idea, but they couldn't lose the business. He'd ended his military career to help keep his father's legacy alive. Besides, he needed the campgrounds. Needed to be in a place where someone wouldn't drive over a mine or trip a wire and blow themselves up.

"I looked into loans. We'd dig our hole deeper owing interest." Brody faced Zach. "The only option left is to sign with *Celebrity Trials.*"

Shit. Zach's stomach knotted as his mind raced. He'd pretty much nixed that chance, but he'd find a better way out.

Think.

Think.

"I have a solution," Zach said.

"What?" Levi asked.

"I've worked on a dozen projects for my friends. They'll help us with this one. We can get materials dirt cheap from Restore, the place where businesses donate their excess supplies. It won't cost near what the contractors charge," Zach said.

Brody shook his head. "That's risky, relying on other people. There will be liability issues if we don't use licensed contractors, and what if the store doesn't have the materials?"

"These aren't just people, they're my buddies." Zach gripped the armrest. Blood brothers, who stood beside each other no matter what. "They run their own businesses now, so they're legit. They've told me before if we ever needed anything they'd get it for us at cost. Whatever we can't get from Restore, they'll supply."

"I don't like it. The show is sure money. We can't afford to take any chances." Brody said.

"Dammit, Brody. It's not taking a chance. I got this."

"Sorry, it's still a no for me."

Zach's ears rang. Control-freak Brody needed to step back and let him handle the repairs. When would his brother ever trust him? "You better reconsider because the production company won't pick here."

"They already did. They called this morning and want this location." Brody sat back in his chair.

Levi pumped a fist in the air. "Hot damn."

Zach's blood pressure zoomed, and he jumped to his feet. "No freaking way. That crew couldn't get out of here fast enough."

Brody's eyes narrowed. "Why?"

Busted.

"Doesn't matter," Zach said. "It's not happening. End of discussion."

Brody thumped the folder. "I'm not excited about it either, but it's this or risk closing down."

"Not true. My plan will work." Zach crossed his arms.

"Stop being a buzzkill." Levi nudged Zach. "The production will bring in droves of people."

"No freaking way I'm having my area turned into a circus. You love the idea so much, let them film at the marina."

"I told you before I'm down with that." Levi clasped his hands together. "I'd be happy to show Crystal how to handle a worm."

"Knock it off, Levi. Not everything is a joke." Brody sighed. "They specified camping. It's not up to us."

"Too bad. I'm out of here." Zach took a step toward the door.

"Not so fast." Brody rose, towering over the desk. "You know the deal. We need to vote on whether to sign with them."

Zach spun on his heel. "Like hell. The campgrounds are my territory."

"You agreed to this arrangement. Majority rules. I vote yes. Levi?"

"Sorry, Zach. I'm in."

Blood pounded in Zach's head, and he fisted his hands. This was going to be a complete shit show.

Chapter Five

C rystal fumed on the whole trip back to Stone Island Park. The producers had refused to consider any other location after watching the films. They'd loved Crystal's reactions to all the hidden horrors awaiting her at what she deemed to be a camper's version of Jurassic Park. Despite her protests, she had no say in the final decision. Sick bastards.

Like before, Trevor had set up ahead of time and stood by his truck, waiting for them. Sydney parked next to a cement slab with a pile of camping gear on top.

Crystal would have to figure out what to do with all that stuff. The YouTube videos she'd seen showed a million different ways to set up camps. She'd never gotten around to reading the rules and safety *missive* Zach had sent them because she was sure they wouldn't pick the location. It would take her a year to plow through it.

"I can't believe I have to deal with that cocky jerk, Zach."

"I'm not his biggest fan either," Sydney said. "Everyone's pissed we had to cut all of the shoot last week since he won't let us use any footage of him on the show."

"Whose fault is that? Shouldn't you have gotten permission to film him ahead of time?"

"I don't need you to tell me how to do my job." Sydney snatched her purse and threw her keys inside. "Most people are eager to be on television."

Grizzly wasn't most people. With his lack of social skills, the man belonged in the wilds. He gave new meaning to the word condescending. How dare he chastise Crystal for not being prepared? She wasn't a Girl Scout.

She'd worn the same glitzy outfit as in the last shoot since they couldn't use that scene. Her fans needed to see her glammed up before she turned into "frontier woman" for the film.

The rumble of an engine grew louder, and Zach emerged from the woods riding his UTV. Once again, he wore camo pants, an olive T-shirt, and those mirrored sunglasses. Did he even own any other clothes?

Crystal's pulse quickened. Two cups of coffee weren't near enough fuel to deal with the guy. She faced Sydney. "How are we going to make this show if you can't film him?"

"When he's in the area working, Trevor will keep him off camera. Zach shouldn't interact with you much. He's not supposed to help you unless there's a safety issue."

Crystal snorted. That might be everything she did from the size of his list.

Zach hopped out of his vehicle and grabbed a clipboard from the back. Crystal's gaze stalled on his tight butt as he bent over the fender. Heat brewed low in her belly. The man infuriated her and so did her schoolgirl responses to him. She cursed under her breath and focused on her feet, making sure she stood in an ant-free zone.

When Zach's boots thumped in front of her, she glanced up.

"Are you kidding me?" He thwacked the clipboard against his thigh. "Still wearing a miniskirt and halter top? Did you listen to anything I said last time? Read the manual I sent?"

Crystal's nerves ignited at his patronizing tone. He had no right to treat her like a child. Did he have any idea what it felt like to be talked down to like some newbie? She had a reputation to restore and had to look the part.

She pointed to her feet. "Closed-toed heels, standing on the cement slab. What more do you want?"

He pinched the bridge of his nose, causing his biceps to bulge, and her traitorous eyes to stare at it. She shivered and ran her tongue across her lips.

A breeze blew, and his head snapped up. "Are you wearing perfume?"

"Yeah. It's my signature scent, Desire." A fan favorite before her popularity had plummeted and her sales followed. Her shoulders tensed. She needed to win back her popularity. One and done with this stupid reality show, and hopefully she'd get her life back.

"No perfume. It attracts animals."

"Apparently not bears." She couldn't resist.

"What?" Zach blew out a breath. "Never mind. Bottom line is we follow rules here. I can't have other people in danger from your reckless behavior."

"If you think wearing perfume is risky, you must not know much about danger. Might want to get out more and see what real threats are in the world."

He stilled. A vein ticked under his jaw.

"We don't want to take up anymore of your time, Zach. What do you need from us?" Sydney asked.

He continued to face Crystal for a long moment, then snatched the paperwork from his clipboard and handed it to Sydney. "This is a list of the supplies and camping equipment we've provided. Brody invoiced and billed the production company. I need your signature."

"Sure." Sydney signed the sheet.

Zach kept his focus on Sydney and pointed to the two vacant tent sites. "The campers coming here this week know about the film and signed waivers. We've sectioned off this area so the day-trippers won't get in the way. If anyone from the set goes outside of here, though, all bets are off."

"Understood." Sydney nodded.

He turned and walked away, his back rigid.

What a jerk. Crystal's temper simmered. "Hey."

Zach stopped and turned. "You talking to me?"

"Yup." She tapped her foot on the ground. "I haven't done anything to deserve your rude, dismissive behavior. You're giving southern people a bad reputation."

His nostrils flared, and he arched an eyebrow. With a slight shake of his head, he continued toward his UTV.

She huffed out a breath and dug her nails into her palms. No one dismissed her like that. Asshole. Maybe since he didn't want them there, he'd avoid her and make life easier. The less she dealt with him, the better.

Chapter Six

Zach grabbed the tools he needed from the side-by-side and headed to the campsite next to Crystal's pad. Damn his brothers for rejecting his plan and signing on the show. Now he had to deal with the ditz for two months. That comment about him knowing nothing about danger burned him up.

He glanced up from the spigot he needed to fix.

Several yards away, Trevor stood beside Crystal on the cement slab of her site, pointing to the places where he'd mounted cameras. "I set up the live feeds to capture what happens here, and we'll sort through what we want to use."

Zach set his teeth. Even though their contract specified they couldn't use any footage of him, the asshats would still be able to see everything he did in the designated area. He was screwed. Easy for Brody and Levi to sign up for shit when their every move wouldn't be recorded.

Crystal nodded. "So outside of here I'm not on camera?"

"Right. I'll be shooting film on location for other scenes."

Trevor focused his camera on Crystal as Sydney held up some sort of whiteboard with words and numbers. Must be what they used at the beginning of each scene, Zach guessed.

He walked to the side of the cement slab and knelt beside the spigot. As he removed the nut to check the valve stem, Crystal strutted across the lot, dragging a hot-pink designer suitcase on freaking wheels. She had one of those fruity, hard-seltzer cans in one hand and stopped to face the camera. With a big grin, she took a sip. Her bright red lips touched the rim, and she tilted her head back, exposing a slender neck.

His mouth went dry. He jerked his gaze back to the fixture, yanked the nut off, and pulled out the stem.

Water fire-hosed him right in the face.

Son of a bitch, he'd forgotten to close the shut-off valve. Crystal had distracted him, and he *never* got distracted. That's how people got hurt or worse. With a string of curses, he raced to the shut-off lever and slammed it down.

A giggle floated through the air, and he turned. Crystal grinned, tipped the frou-frou drink as if to toast him, and took another sip.

His blood pressure spiked, and he gave her his best glare.

Her blue eyes fired lasers at him as she held his gaze.

She wasn't intimidated. Maybe she had more grit than he'd thought.

Water dripped from his nose, and he cursed again. No way a combat engineer should have forgotten something as simple as shutting off the water. Training, training, training. Safety first. Follow the rules. He wiped his face with the bottom of his T-shirt in disgust and went back to the spigot.

Crystal and her entourage, be it small, approached. She took another show-off sip of the drink, and her spiked heel sunk into a soft spot in the grass. She teetered and fell to the ground on her side. Her miniskirt rode up, revealing a perfectly-shaped ass framed by a bright-pink thong that matched the color of the luggage.

Sydney's hand flew to her mouth as she smothered a laugh.

Trevor grinned as he kept the camera focused on Crystal.

Assholes.

Not that Crystal was Zach's favorite person, but she might be hurt, and all they cared about was the show.

"Stop filming," he yelled as he jogged to her. She'd managed to flip her skirt back down over her butt. "You okay?"

"Yeah."

He offered a hand and helped her up.

Her eyes widened, and she swallowed. "Th-thanks. I didn't expect...I mean..."

His fingers tingled where her small, soft hand rested. He let go and took a step back. How did she make him buzz like that?

He cleared his throat, taking a quick survey of her. She wasn't bleeding and didn't seem to be in pain, so probably nothing to worry about.

She had a splotch of mud on her glittered halter and a smudge of dirt smeared across her nose. He resisted the urge to wipe it because he wasn't about to touch her again.

It pissed him off they'd kept rolling the cameras, but she had signed up for the reality show, knowing they would film all her mishaps. Not much pride in a person who would trade their dignity for money.

After pulling the broken heel out of the clay soil with her fake, fire-engine-red fingernails, she inspected it. "These shoes cost a fortune. Is there a repair shop anywhere near here?"

Whatever moment they'd just shared was over. He snorted. "Sure, right next to the farm stand."

She thrust a hand on her hip. "There's no reason to be—"

"Crystal, we need to stay on schedule." Sydney tapped her watch.

"I'll get out of your way." Zach returned to the water fixture and dug around in his toolbox. He stole a glance at Crystal, who hobbled closer, opened her suitcase, tucked the broken shoe inside, and strapped on some sort of wedge ones. More heels? Total insanity. What else had she packed? Bad enough he had the image of her sweet ass in that thong burned into his brain. He didn't need to see the lacy bras, silky shirts, and strips of what might pass for underwear all out on display.

The rumble of a motorcycle grew louder as Levi rode up and

dismounted near them. He hardly ever visited the campgrounds, always busy at the marina. Everyone turned to look at him, and Trevor held the camera up again.

Must have come to get on film, that ham. He'd signed a waiver and encouraged them to use as many shots of him as they wanted. With a big grin on his face, he stopped in front of Crystal and held out a hand. "Hey. Heard you were here. Welcome. I'm Levi."

"You're the one who does the boat stuff, right?" She shook his hand.

"Guilty as charged." He raised his sunglasses and checked her out from head to toe, his gaze stopping on her smudged shirt. "Are you all right?"

Glancing down, she frowned. "Ugh. I didn't see that. I fell."

"I'm sure it will wash out. You okay?" Levi leaned in, his voice full of concern.

Zach yanked a washer out of the fixture. Leaning in, really? Did any woman fall for that?

"I'm fine. My shoe isn't, though. And it's my favorite pair." She bent to fish the broken heel out of her suitcase, and Levi slid his shades back down. No doubt so he could check out her ass.

Zach focused his attention back on the spigot.

"That looks like a clean break. I'm sure it can be fixed," Levi said.

"Zach said there was a shoe repair place next to the farm stand. I don't think that's the case."

Levi laughed. "No, but I can get it fixed for you."

"Really?" She nibbled her lip. "Do you think it will cost much?"

"Nah. It's a simple repair. I'll send it out to the online shoe shop, and they'll ship it back."

Zach's face heated. What horse shit. An online repair shop—his ass. Levi was making stuff up as he went along. He probably had boat glue in the marina he planned to use. Regardless, Crystal was buying his BS. Why was she worried about the repair cost? Didn't she have closets full of money all over her penthouse?

"I'd be grateful, and of course I'll pay for it. I didn't pack many shoes. Had to leave room for clothes." She waved a hand at the open suitcase and flipped the lid, covering the contents like she'd just realized her lingerie was on display.

Not fast enough.

Levi's grin widened. "I'm happy to help in any way I can."

Zach cursed under his breath and shoved the newly clad valve stem back into the fixture. Unbelievable.

"Hey, bro." Levi glanced at Zach and laughed. "What happened? Did you fall in the lake?"

"Can it. Don't you have work to do?" Zach reassembled the fixture.

"Not when there's a beautiful lady here to distract me." He leaned in again and said loud enough for Zach to hear him, "He tends to be grumpy."

Crystal smiled and said in a soft tone, "I kinda noticed that, but thanks for the warning."

"If you want some fun, I'm your man."

Zach bit back the caustic reply on the tip of his tongue and turned the water shut-off back on. Let them whisper and joke all they wanted. He didn't give a crap.

"You have a smudge on your nose." Levi touched his own.

"I do?" Crystal wiped the wrong side. "Is it gone?"

"No. It's... may I?" Levi held his hand up.

She shrugged. "I guess. Sure."

"Right here." Levi wiped the mud with his thumb. "There you go, perfect."

"Thanks."

In less than five minutes, Levi had managed to sweet talk her, play the hero offering to fix her shoe, and now *touch* her. That simple gesture raised Zach's hackles. Because damn it, *he* wanted to touch her. And that pissed him off to hell and back.

"Have you seen the island yet?" Levi asked.

"No. I have a map, though."

"A map?"

"Yeah, it was on the top of the pile of paperwork from him."
Crystal gave Zach the stink eye.

"No doubt. I bet you also got an encyclopedia-sized book of
rules to go with it?"

"Right? Who can read all that?"

If seeing red was real, Zach would be looking through a bloody
haze. Levi needed to get off his back and out of his business. He had
a thing or two to tell his little brother in private. "Levi?"

"Yeah?"

"A word with you after you're done here," Zach commanded.
Not a question.

Crystal brushed at the mud on her halter top, pressing the material against her body, and Zach's brain froze.

Levi's gaze darted from him to Crystal and back. A shit-eating
grin lit up his face. "Well, isn't this going to be fun?"

"What?" Crystal and Zach asked at the same time.

Zach scowled.

Levi tipped his head. "You want a word with me, Zach? Sure,
I'll climb into the ring."

Smart-ass. Damn straight there was going to be some butt
kicking.

Levi turned back to Crystal. "Want a tour of the island on my
motorcycle?"

"Can I do that?" Crystal asked Sydney.

Sydney hesitated and then agreed. "Yeah. We might be able to
drum up some drama with a love interest. I like it."

Crystal brought a hand to her chest and gestured to Levi. "No, I
don't want to put him in that position. We just met and—"

"Are you kidding? It'll be fun. All for the show. No worries."
Levi reached into his pocket and pulled out a pack of gum. "You
want a piece?"

"Watermelon? That's my favorite." She took the stick he held
out to her.

He slowly stripped the silver wrap off his and folded the gum into his mouth, sending a smug smirk in Zach's direction. "Mine too."

Total jerkoff.

"Yo, bro," Levi yelled.

"What?" Zach smacked a hand on the spigot. "Can't you see I'm busy?"

"Mom called again about the cat."

Zach waved a hand. "I got it. I'm taking her to the vet at four."

"She also said something about the nursery."

"I figured as much." He shook his head but couldn't stop the smile that tugged at the corner of his mouth. "Got that too."

Mom and her flowers. Zach's heart twinged. That's what made her happy since his dad had passed. Gardening and her fourteen-year-old cat with one blue eye and one brown. Zach would do whatever it took, even if it meant loading plants on the flat cart and swapping them out every time she changed her mind.

"Ready for a ride?" Levi faced Crystal.

"Sure," Crystal said. But she cocked her head and kept her gaze on Zach.

"Let's go, then."

Trevor moved closer with his camera aimed at her. She climbed onto the motorcycle and wrapped arms around Levi. Her skirt hiked up, exposing more of her toned, creamy thighs.

Zach sucked in a breath as a wave of heat rushed south.

Levi gunned the throttle several times, and Crystal hugged him tighter.

"Wait." Crystal pulled her phone out and took a selfie of them.

Zach's patience snapped as his gut wrenched. He yelled over the sound of the motorcycle, "Helmets."

Levi grinned and called back, "Not required in this state. Don't worry. I'll take care of your girl."

Zach flinched. His girl?

She wasn't his girl. She wasn't his anything. She was a pain in the ass. And now she was the new reality show love interest of his younger brother.

Sydney yelled to Trevor, "You got all that, right? The fall and her bare ass in the thong?"

"Hell yeah." He gave her a thumbs-up. "That's gonna boost ratings."

Levi rode off with Crystal, Trevor filming from behind on foot.

Zach's gut twisted in a sick way. How could Crystal allow herself to be publicly humiliated? He ran a hand down his face and sighed. She had to know people would make fun of her. That tore at him, but it was out of his hands. Still, he should at least tell her how happy Trevor and Sydney were to capture her ass on film.

He'd talk to her as soon as she got back.

Chapter Seven

When Crystal returned from the ride with Levi, Zach was nowhere in sight. Just as well, because she'd had her fill of him for one day. She and Levi had been gone longer than she'd expected, since he had stopped at the marina to show her the place. He'd also been nice enough to offer her the use of his bicycle anytime she wanted. Interesting that he'd quit flirting with her once they'd left the campsite. That was a good thing. She wasn't there to strike up any romance, and she'd enjoyed the tour.

She checked her social media sites and grinned. The pictures she'd posted of her glam outfit were trending. People asked about her halter top and miniskirt from the first camping day. Where had she bought them and what brand? Then again, others left comments about her Rodeo Drive clothes and mentioned they weren't camping attire. Either way, everyone seemed eager to see her next post. Hey, at least she had some followers again.

Changing into sneakers, she sighed. The tent needed to be set up before dark. As much fun as she'd had with Levi while they'd motored around the island, thoughts of Zach had kept hi-jacking her brain. She'd been fine loathing him until that comment about his mother and the cat. And something about his smile at the mention of the nursery had gotten to her.

Damn it. He had a heart after all, and hers pinched.

No. The guy was a jerk. She shook her head.

She frowned at the concrete slab. Way too hard. Eying the grassier ground near the lake, she grabbed the tent and stakes. She'd set up closer to the water on the soft sand.

After she hauled the equipment down the slope, she fired up YouTube. She found a video that demonstrated pitching a tent similar to hers. Sweat stung her eyes as she pounded stakes into the hard, clay ground, ripping off a fake nail in the process. So much for soft, sandy soil. She'd have to lose the nails for this gig. Angst over how she'd keep up appearances made her nerves twitch. Good thing she'd done her glam shots earlier.

She smacked a mosquito on her leg. Blood smeared, and she cringed.

Gah.

A small welt formed, itching. She'd better hurry inside with all her gear before they ate her alive. She scurried into the tent, zipped the flap shut, and rubbed her hands down her legs. Who the hell did this for fun?

She knew someone who did. Her friend Jenna, the only one who hadn't turned on her.

Crystal longed to see a friendly face and vent. Jenna had always been there for her. They'd bonded as kids on a show in San Diego, where Jenna's Navy SEAL father was stationed. Kind of amazing with all the moving around Jenna did that she'd kept in touch. But they both had a desperate need for a real friend, and they'd been through hell together on that program.

Even though Jenna was an adventure guide who spent a lot of time in remote locations with no cell service, she managed to talk to Crystal on a regular basis. She sat on the floor and clicked her contact number.

Jenna answered, adjusted the angle of her phone to center her face on the screen, and smiled. "Hey, girl. Great timing. I'm off the grid starting tomorrow."

As always, Jenna had that wild-child look, with her untamed red hair falling in ringlets around her face. The sight of her and the sound of her voice eased the lonely ache in Crystal's chest. "Where are you?"

"Canada. We're hiking and camping along the Saint Lawrence River. It's gorgeous here." Jenna turned the phone around and scanned the area.

The sky was hurt-your-eyes-bright-blue over beautiful, turquoise water. "That's as pretty as the Caribbean."

Jenna's face came back on the screen. "Only way, way colder. We're having a blast, though. How are things with you?"

Crystal held up her hand to the phone camera and wiggled her fingers. "I'm down to nine nails, my leg is bleeding from bug bites, and the guy who runs the campgrounds is this buff, by-the-book, condescending, arrogant ass that I just want to—"

"Kiss?"

Crystal jerked her head back. "Kiss? Where'd that come from?"

"You started with buff." Jenna leaned back and flexed a biceps, laughing.

She had a point. A really annoying point. "No. I'd rather throttle him."

"I'm dying to see what he looks like. Send me a pic."

"I don't have one. He won't allow any film of him shared, and I sure as hell didn't take any pictures."

"All right." Jenna leaned in closer. "You okay, aside from mister-know-it-all?"

Crystal glanced from her torn nail to all her gear piled up in a corner. "Yeah, this just sucks."

"I know it's not your thing, but what choice do you have?" Her eyes softened. "After your mother—"

"Let's not talk about her. That will depress me more."

Jenna gave a slow nod. "Fair enough. I wish I could be there with you."

"I'd love the company." Crystal stood. "I need to go. Thanks for the chat, and don't fall off any cliffs or get trampled by a moose."

"You know I'm better than that. Hang in there, girl." Jenna winked and waved goodbye.

Crystal swiped to hang up and drummed her fingers on a knee. Jenna thought Crystal wanted to kiss Zach? Crazy talk. No freaking way. Yet, when he'd wiped his face with the hem of his shirt after being hosed, she'd checked out his ripped abs. Who wouldn't? It meant nothing.

Frogs croaked until they reached a crescendo that hurt her ears. She covered them and squeezed her eyes shut. How was she ever going to sleep with all the noise?

A lone, long howl made her stomach vault. Maybe a coyote? She had to pee, and now that she'd moved closer to the lake, the restroom was a hike. Ugh. She peered out the tiny, screened window of the tent. No wild animals in sight, but she couldn't see far in the dark.

Looked like she'd be peeing in the woods.

She grabbed her phone and brought up the missive Zach had emailed to her. When she got back, she'd read it after all.

Especially the section on wild animals and bears.

Cold water seeped down Crystal's back, waking her as rain battered the top and sides of her tent. She sat up. Her butt and legs sank into the sopping wet sleeping bag. With a gasp, she jumped to her feet and whacked her head on the top of the tent.

Stupid small space.

Water dripped from her silky nightgown, and her heart raced. Everything she owned was in the flooding tent. In the dim morning light peeking through the tent cracks, she spied her suitcase and yanked it off the ground.

Too late.

The sides were already water stained and gritty. She had to get to the restroom to wash the clothes inside, or they'd be ruined. Her glam-shot outfit would be destroyed.

She slapped on her flip-flops and unzipped the tent. Rain pelted her face, and the wind whipped against her while she struggled to zip the flap with one hand, the other holding the suitcase.

Water rushed down the slope in a torrent. The hum of a vehicle sounded in the distance. Headlights shined over the top of the hill. Squinting into the rain, she trudged forward, but her foot slipped off the slick flip-flop, and she fell to the ground, face-forward with a *thud*.

The bag went flying. Muddy, cool water gushed down the front of her nighty, and pain radiated from her ribs to her shoulders. Shit, that was going to leave a mark.

"Are you all right?" Zach called from the top of the slope.

Before she could answer, he'd raced down and squatted beside her. "Are you hurt?"

She pushed off the ground and sucked in a breath. No searing pain, so she mustn't have broken any bones. She shivered and wrapped her arms around herself. "I-I'm fine."

A beam of light blinded her eyes, and she blinked. "What are you doing?"

"Checking your pupils to see if they're dilated. You might have a concussion."

Okay, this guy was out of control. "I didn't even hit my head."

"Well, I don't know how many times you fell." He lowered the flashlight beam to her feet. "Flip-flops? Seriously?"

Through white spots dotting her vision, she focused on his rain parka and boots. Of course, he was prepared. "What are you even doing out here?"

"I check on all the campers when there's a storm," he said.

The rain continued to drench her, and the wind picked up, causing her to yell over the noise. "Can you please get out of my way?"

He shook his head. "Where's your rain gear?"

Hot energy surged through her body as her patience snapped. "I didn't ask for your help, and I need to get my clothes to the restroom."

"Well, you aren't going to make it up there in those shoes."

Crystal's body shook harder, her bones chilling. "Leave me alone. I got this."

She reached for her suitcase and slipped again. This time she did catch herself, but both hands sunk into the mud.

Zach cursed under his breath and scooped her up in his arms. "You are the biggest pain in the ass I've ever dealt with."

She sputtered, "Let me down."

"Nope. This is now a rescue mission." Zach took strong, sure steps up the slope, each one bouncing her off his hard chest. The heat from his body warmed her even through his parka as her agitation smoldered.

Lightning flashed, followed by a loud boom of thunder a mere second after.

Startled, she gripped his neck and buried her face in the crook of it under his hood, shielded from the rain. His arms tightened around her, securing her to his body.

Yikes that strike was close, and why did he have to smell so good? She inhaled the scent of pine, musk, and the fresh outdoors.

As soon as they reached the restroom, he plopped her down in front of the door like a UPS delivery and stepped back. His hood shadowed his face. Emotionless, no doubt.

Just a "rescue mission." Like she wasn't a real person. No feelings or attachments. Only she'd caught the concern in his voice when he'd checked her condition. Still, she hadn't asked for his help.

He turned his head to face the woods, and she glanced down. The drenched pink nighty left nothing to the imagination. Mud-caked and all. She cringed and crossed her arms to cover her breasts.

He waved a hand in the direction of her tent. "Why on earth did you set up at the bottom of a hill? That's on the fall line of the slope and why the concrete slab is up here."

"I had my reasons. Not your problem. And you aren't supposed to help me anyway. You're in breach of contract, and Sydney's gonna see that on the video."

That should shut him up.

He scoffed. "For the record, I'm allowed to intervene in safety matters and you falling on your ass every two steps in a mudslide qualifies as one. You're a danger to yourself."

Screw him. She didn't need his attention or approval.

Another blast of wind caused her teeth to chatter, and she shivered so hard her whole body shook. "Y-You—"

"Enough. Go inside and take a warm shower. I'll grab your bag." He stomped toward the hill, where she'd dropped the suitcase.

Ugh, that flippant, arrogant asshole. He had no right to order her around. She yanked the door open and tried to slam it, but the stupid thing closed slowly.

She stopped cold at her reflection in the mirror. Holy crap, she looked like a drowned flamingo. Good thing the lighting was poor in the storm. The rain should have blurred the video recording on the stationary cameras. If Trevor did come up with some footage, Crystal wouldn't approve the usage. She'd have the final say. That way they couldn't embarrass her on film.

She squinted at the light shining in through the bathroom window. Zach had to have gotten a good look at her up close.

Her cheeks heated. Even though he'd averted his gaze at the bathroom entrance, he'd still carried her up the freaking hill and damn it, she'd clung to him like a frightened kitten. She should have forced him to put her down instead of breathing in his scent and burying her face against his warm neck.

Maybe between the wild weather and the slippery slope he hadn't noticed she'd curled into his arms. That's all she could hope for.

She made her way around the corner to the shower stalls and turned on the water. While she waited for it to warm up, the bathroom door opened, and Zach called out, "Not coming in, just leaving your bag."

Thump.

Maybe she'd find something dry in it to wear. No telling.

She took her time in the shower, enjoying the warm water. As she rinsed her hair, a knock sounded on the door.

"Me again, dropping off another bag. Still not coming in," Zach called.

A softer thud this time. What was that?

She wrung out her hair and peeked around the corner at the vacant bathroom. Her suitcase was on the floor next to a half-filled, black trash bag.

Dripping wet and shivering again, she dashed across the room, snatched up both, and hurried back to the shower stall area. She unzipped the case and stuck her hand inside, rummaging through her clothes in search of anything dry.

Nope. All wet.

Her stomach sank, and goosebumps formed on her arms.

She should have gotten a hard-shell suitcase, but the bright pink canvas one had called to her. She'd never expected to need a weatherproof bag when she'd bought one a year ago.

With shaking fingers, she opened the black trash bag and almost wept at the sight of dry towels. She wrapped one around her and made a turban for her hair with the other.

Bundled up, she pulled out an olive-drab T-shirt and a black pair of sweatpants. She held them to her cold face, and her heart tripped.

She knew that scent.

She should put the clothes back in the bag. She should tell him she didn't need his charity. She should stop smelling the dang shirt and fantasizing about someone who annoyed the ever-living shit out of her.

And yet, she stood there, holding the shirt.

Grizzly made it hard for her to hate him when he showed his soft side.

Chapter Eight

Zach finished his morning survey loop of the park and stopped near Crystal's campsite. None of the other campers had had any issue with the storm last night. Just defiant Crystal, who'd decided to pitch a tent at the bottom of a hill.

It would have served her right to be miserable in cold, wet clothes until the temps heated up, but that was not the way he ran his camp. He helped whoever needed a hand.

The producers might have more humiliating footage of Crystal if anything on their cameras was of use. He'd waited as long as he could for her to get back from the motorcycle ride to talk to her yesterday but had run out of time. At this point, what did it matter that Trevor had footage of Crystal's thong when she'd fallen? She had to realize they would continue filming her mishaps. Clearly, that was what she signed up for and didn't care.

He frowned. That flash of lightning and thunderous boom had scared the shit out of Crystal. The urge to protect and comfort her had kicked in. And when she'd gripped him and pressed her freezing cold body against him, he'd held her closer.

Damn, she got under his skin. What was it about her? She'd argue with him about the color of mud just for the sake of it. And scared as she was about the wild animals and storms, she'd still pushed back when he'd tried to help her. It hadn't been until he'd carried her up the hill that she'd let go of the fake bravado and showed her vulnerable side.

She'd sure doubled down once he'd let go of her.

Zach froze. He shut his eyes and pressed a finger to his forehead. When was the last time a boom of thunder hadn't shaken him to the core? Any sound that resonated like a bomb going off triggered him.

Maybe he'd been so engaged in mission-mode, trying to help her, that he hadn't reacted.

He took a deep breath and hopped into his side-by-side. No time to think about this stuff, he had a job to do.

He parked behind the restroom to stay off the cameras, and emptied a dumpster, chucking the trash bags into his trailer when Sydney arrived. Crystal entered his line of vision as she sauntered across the lot in front of the bathroom, wearing his T-shirt and sweatpants. She'd rolled up the cuffs, cinched the waist with some sort of hair clip, and tied a knot in the front of his T-shirt.

Something stirred in his belly at the sight of her in his clothes. He'd been sure she'd toss them aside. No fashion statement in that outfit, and yet she somehow pulled it off.

She still wore those dreaded flip-flops, and his mouth curved into a smile despite himself.

Stubborn woman.

Zach grabbed his pesticide sprayer and began treating the area.

Sydney got out of the car and marched to Crystal. "What the hell went on this morning? Zach was on the site. We can't use the recording, and that was good stuff."

His throat burned. Good stuff? Those assholes didn't give a rat's ass about whether Crystal might have been hurt. They only wanted to capture as many humiliating and embarrassing gaffes as they could.

Crystal tightened the knot on the camo shirt and shrugged. "Zach said it was some sort of safety issue. No idea."

Sydney snorted. "That's pushing it." She gestured to Crystal's outfit. "Are these men's clothes? Did Zach give them to you?"

"Another safety issue. Health-related." Crystal tapped her chest. "I could catch pneumonia and die if I don't stay warm. That would end the show, and no one wants that to happen."

Zach grinned. Smart-ass. That was his girl.

Shit.

His girl? Where the hell had that come from?

A motorcycle revved, and Levi pulled into the lot. "Hey. Checking to see if everyone's all right after the storm."

Zach grunted. What a poser. A bit late to the scene.

A slow, calculated smile formed on Sydney's face. "We're good. Things just got better."

The sprayer hissed air, so Zach headed back to the side-by-side to mix up another batch. After he refilled the tank, he rounded the corner of the restroom. Trevor had his back to Zach, with the camera pointing at Crystal and Levi. Sydney had stepped out of the picture.

"Things sure got a little wild here in the storm last night, huh?" Levi leaned against his motorcycle, facing Crystal.

"That's an understatement. I've never been that close to a lightning strike." Crystal rubbed her arms. "And the rain flooded everything. My clothes are drenched."

"They'll dry out fast. And if not, you're rocking this outfit." Levi pushed off the motorcycle and tugged the knot Crystal had made in the shirt. "I'd never expect you to look so cute wearing men's clothes."

"Well, I appreciate the loan." Crystal tilted her head, and the corners of her lips turned up.

Zach stilled. What was wrong with her? People would think she and Levi had sex with his talk about a wild night and her acting like the clothes were his. Did she have no self-respect?

Levi rested a hand on Crystal's arm. "The important thing is you're okay."

"Like you said, clothes will dry." She shrugged.

"I gotta go, I have a pontoon tour soon, but my mom's a big fan of yours, and she makes a huge dinner every Sunday. We all go. If you're allowed off the set for a meal, I'd love for you to come tonight."

Zach shook his head as blood rushed to his brain. Unbelievable. Now Levi was inviting her to the family dinner and making up stuff about their mom being a fan. What BS. She only watched gardening shows and an occasional Hallmark movie.

"I'll have to check with the producers." Crystal glanced at Sydney, who nodded and gave a thumbs up.

Levi beamed. "Looks like you're cleared. I'll swing by to get you at five."

Trevor filmed Levi as he rode off and then lowered the camera.

Crystal's shoulders slumped, and her face fell.

"We won't be able to film that dinner tonight," Trevor said to Sydney.

"Don't need to. All that matters is he asked her out, and she's going."

Seething, Zach pumped the sprayer hard. What an idiot he'd been, feeling sorry for Crystal. She played everyone. He paused to wipe the sweat off his face and caught her gaze.

She swallowed, took a step in his direction, then turned back to Sydney.

"Wait. We can't use that. I...I changed my mind."

Zach snapped the sprayer arm into the side slot and headed back to his side-by-side.

"Don't go, Zach. I need to talk to you," Crystal yelled.

Chapter Nine

Crystal jogged after Zach. By the time she reached the back of the building, he'd pulled away. He probably hadn't heard her over the sound of the engine.

Damn.

Her heart fell into the dust trail.

She'd had no idea he was working in the area and would see that scene with Levi. Zach's red face and clenched jaw told her all she needed to know. The man was furious. He'd gone out of his way to loan her his clothes, and she'd given all the credit to Levi. She'd had a good reason, though. If Zach would only listen to her, he might understand.

What a mess. She should cancel the dinner plans, but maybe she'd have a chance to talk to him there. Levi made it sound like the whole family attended.

Only one way to find out. She texted Levi and asked him to pick her up outside of the designated film area before they went to his mom's. She didn't want their conversation to be recorded. He agreed and they chose a place to meet at five.

When it was time, she jogged to the spot and sat on a curb. She pulled out her phone, clicked on her social media sites, and gasped. Wow. More followers. A lot more. And the last picture she'd posted, the selfie of her and Levi on the motorcycle, had gone viral. Some people commented on her attire and how hot she looked, and others argued that the clothes weren't appropriate for camping. Who knew she'd start a controversy and get a following by posting camping pictures? Hey, any attention was good publicity.

She flashed back to Zach's expression as she'd rode off with Levi, and her mood dampened.

A motorcycle engine grew louder, and Crystal stood and dusted off her jean shorts.

Levi came to a stop. "Hey, pretty lady, what's up with the sad face?"

"Thanks for picking me up here. I wanted to talk to you in private. I feel horrible. I never should have done that scene with you. I apologize for putting you in such a hard spot. I was just trying to keep your family out of trouble."

Levi hopped off the motorcycle. "I know. Same here."

"Zach won't even talk to me now."

"Does that bother you?"

"Yeah." Why? She didn't want Zach around in the first place. All he did was criticize her, so she should be happy he took off. And she could do without the physical reactions she had to him. Only that betrayed look on his face haunted her.

"I know how to cheer you up." Levi reached into a pouch behind the seat and pulled out a package of Twizzlers. "Want a piece?"

Crystal smiled. "What are you, the candy man?"

"Hey, sugar works." Levi grinned and handed her a rope. He whipped a Twizzler in the air and leaned against the motorcycle. "You know, Zach has a thing for you."

Crystal's stomach flipped. That couldn't be true. All they did was argue all the time. Yet, he still managed to make her pulse race and her breath unsteady whenever they were together.

"I don't know what you're talking about. He doesn't even like me, much less have a thing for me. I think he was mad about me suggesting I wore your clothes. That doesn't even make sense. Why would he care?"

Levi shook his head and sighed. "He's not easy to explain, but you might want to give him a chance."

"I'm hoping I'll get that opportunity at your mom's."

"One thing you can count on is Zach never disappoints Mom. He'll be there. Sorry about the way things worked out today too, but it was kinda fun to poke the bear."

Crystal squinched her face. What did that mean?

"Anything else you want to talk about? I'm all ears."

"No. I think I've said enough, but thanks."

Levi gestured to the motorcycle, and she climbed on. They drove a short distance to a blue cottage with a farm stand by the road. A painted wooden sign with pictures of peaches, tomatoes, cucumbers, and squash read, "Fresh Produce."

Crystal pointed to the table. "I guess this is your mom's?"

"Yup. She's quite the gardener."

A woman came out of the house onto the screened porch, carrying a watering can. She wore overalls, a white shirt with the sleeves rolled up, and a baseball cap. She smiled. "Hi, Levi. Who's your friend?"

Levi trotted up the steps and hugged her. "Mom, this is Crystal, the star of that reality show they're filming on the island."

"Welcome, I'm Erin." She wrapped an arm around Crystal and side-hugged her.

Talk about southern hospitality. Crystal awkwardly patted Erin's back.

Erin released her. "I hear you're in the show filming here. I'm sorry, but I don't watch much television. Early to bed, early to rise around here."

Crystal's ego took a direct hit, and her lungs deflated. She reached the new low of being thrilled that someone's mother was still a fan, only to find out not so much.

"What's wrong, Crystal? You look like somebody just mowed

down your petunia patch." Erin set down the watering can and peered up at her, her brown eyes radiating warmth and concern.

Crystal's throat swelled. Her mother had never looked at her that way. Always bleary-eyed from drugs or alcohol. Crystal shook it off and sent the feelings packing. Something she had plenty of practice doing.

"I'm fine." She elbowed Levi. "Big fan?"

Levi winced. "Sorry, but I wanted you to come tonight."

"Why?"

Zach pulled into the driveway on his UTV and shut off the engine. He glanced up at them. His chest rose and fell before he launched out of the vehicle, grabbed a silver tarp from the back, and disappeared around the side of the house.

Levi snatched his phone from his belt and frowned at the screen. "There's a problem at the marina. I need to run."

Erin reached for his arm. "Oh no, you just got here. At least take a to-go plate. I'll make—"

"No time, Mom. Emergency." He gave her a quick peck on the cheek.

"Sorry, Crystal, I'm sure Zach can give you a ride back to the camp." Levi bounded down the steps and hopped onto his motorcycle.

The bike roared down the street, and Zach came back out front. He stopped short and frowned in Levi's direction.

Shaking his head, Zach approached them.

Crystal straightened her shoulders, her heart beating faster.

Erin called out, "Zach, have you met Crystal?"

"Yes, ma'am." He stopped at the bottom of the steps and waved a hand at the road. "Where the hel—heck did Levi go?"

"Some marina emergency." Erin shrugged. "He said you could take Crystal back to the park."

Zach's eyes slitted. "I don't think so. I'll make other arrangements."

Yup. He was mad all right. Crystal bit her lip and held out the bag with his clothes. "I wanted to return these, and if you have a minute—"

"Leave them on the porch. I'll get them later." He brushed by her and opened the door to the house.

"Zachary Edward Stone, you are being rude to a guest in my home, and I won't have it. I taught you better." Erin planted her hands on her hips.

He paused and turned around.

"Sorry, Mom. Nothing to worry about. There won't be any theatrics *here*."

Her gaze darted between Crystal and Zach, then down the dirt driveway where Levi had high-tailed it out of there.

"I'll set the table now. Anything else you need?" He waited.

"No, but thanks," Erin said.

He went inside and Erin let out a defeated sigh.

Crystal didn't know what to say or do. The moment was awkward.

Erin turned and snapped to attention. "I'm sorry. Where are my manners? Would you like to see the gardens?"

"Sure." Anything to give Zach's blood pressure time to settle.

Erin wandered with her through the gorgeous, well-tended gardens, showing her the plants and vegetables.

"It's beautiful but looks like a lot of work," Crystal said.

"I used to do more. Once my husband passed, I had to cut back. The boys can only help so much, and losing their father hit them hard." Erin's eyes watered, and a pang of sympathy squeezed Crystal's insides. She'd never met her father or lost a loved one, for that matter. Poor Erin.

"I'm sorry for your loss." She stroked the petal of a bright red rose. "I'm glad you have all this."

Erin sighed and nodded. "And my boys. For that I'm blessed." She grabbed Crystal's hand. "Come see one more thing before we go in for supper."

She glanced down at their joined hands, and a wave of warmth washed through her.

A screen door banged, and Crystal turned. Zach stood on the second-story deck of the house, holding a drink. Erin waved and led Crystal across the lawn to a small, red-painted barn. When they entered, the sweet scent of hay wafted in the air. Aside from two stacked bales in the corner, the space was empty.

"I'm still deciding what to do with this place and would love another opinion." Erin let go of Crystal's hand and strolled through the building. "The boys are always thinking of ways for me to bring in extra income. They cleaned and repainted this so I could rent it out as a studio. You probably know more than I do about this kind of thing, given your profession. What do you think?"

Crystal followed Erin, taking time to think before she answered. Leaves rustled in the breeze and birds chirped.

"It's remote and peaceful. An artist would have a quiet space to work." Crystal tilted her head and nodded as an image formed. "I have an eye for photography, and with your gorgeous gardens, this would be a great place for engagement and prom pictures. It could even be a venue for weddings. There's real money in that business."

"Wow. I never thought of that. I'll have to look into all the options."

Zach's silhouette appeared in the doorway, casting a dark shadow from the sun gleaming behind him. "Brody's here, Mom. I think Crystal has taken up enough of your time."

"Okay, great. And stop being grumpy. She's a sweet girl, and you need to mind your manners." Erin pointed a finger at him and walked past. "I'll see you up at the house. Don't dawdle. Brody is always on a schedule."

"We won't be long," Zach said.

Silence engulfed the barn as Erin's footsteps faded.

Crystal's pulse skipped. His mood hadn't improved. "I wanted to talk to you earlier at the park, but you ran away."

"Ran away?" He stepped into the barn. "I didn't run away. I had nothing to say to you after that sham between you and Levi."

"You don't understand. Sydney—"

"No excuses. I know what I saw. I don't give a damn what you say or do with Levi, just don't you dare play my mother," he said in a deep, gravelly tone.

"Play your mother? What are you talking about?" She had been sincere and nice to Erin.

"Stay clear of her. She doesn't understand your type."

"My type?" Her blood heated. "What is my type?"

"The kind of person who doesn't give a crap about her reputation and will lie on camera to get ratings. You're hurting our business, and Levi is clueless. Thank God my mother doesn't watch reality shows."

"Hurting your business? I'm saving your business." She stomped her foot. "Sydney was pissed you carried me up that slope and lent me clothes. She told Levi and me she was going to fine your business for breach of contract if we didn't find a way to cover it."

He crossed his arms, and Crystal took a step closer. "Levi refused at first. He wanted no part of it."

"Well, he got over that fast enough. Either you're a better actress than I thought, or you're into him."

"Why do you care? Are you jealous?"

Zach scoffed. "Hardly, just saying, you both sure played the part."

Her temperature spiked. She took another step and glared up at him. "You need to give your brother more credit. I had to beg him to act the way he did to save your ass because I couldn't stand the thought of you"—she poked Zach's shoulder with her finger—"paying for my stupidity."

That hurt to admit.

Zach captured her hand and held it against his chest, standing stock-still. Tingles radiated up her arm, and tears burned the back of her eyes.

The blinding sun behind him hid his face, but his heart thumped hard under her hand. His warm breath blew across her hot cheeks, and the room shrank.

A light breeze swirled the heated air between them. He gave her hand a gentle squeeze and leaned closer. Now she could see his expression, and it rocked her to the core. His eyes darkened, and his gaze dropped to her lips.

Was he going to kiss her? God help her, she wanted him to. Her knees went weak, and she closed her eyes.

"Dinner's on the table," Erin called from the deck of the house.

Zach dropped Crystal's hand and jerked back with a curse.

Blood rushed to her face. How on earth had she let things go that far? He pushed all her buttons, and she still couldn't resist him.

He shook his head and took a step toward the door. "We're done here."

Humiliation washed over her like a bucket of ice water.

Fine.

As far as she was concerned, that almost-kiss never happened. But she wasn't near done talking to him. Stubborn, judgmental ogre. He should be thanking her for looking out for him.

"Stop right there." She stormed across the barn and blocked his way. "For the record, I'm never signing off on that scene with Levi. I won't let them use film that makes anyone look bad, including me. Sydney can't release footage I don't approve, so it's never going to be aired." Crystal narrowed her eyes. "And it's beyond insulting you think I would ever take advantage of your mother."

She turned her back to him and headed to the barn entrance. When she reached it, she whirled to face him. "One more thing." She jabbed a finger in his direction. "You owe Levi an apology for thinking the worst of him."

She blew her bangs up and squared her shoulders. "*Now*, we're done here."

The door slammed behind her.

Bang.

No soft-close this time.

Satisfying.

To hell with him. She had sneakers on and could jog back to the island. A good way to release some stress. He didn't want her at the family dinner anyhow, and there was no way she'd sit at the same table and make small talk. Unfortunately, she wouldn't have a chance to thank his mother.

She never had a family before and didn't need one now. That man could goad Gandhi to violence.

So exasperating.

At least she'd had her say. Let him wallow in his anger.

Her shoes slapped against the pavement, and heat from the black asphalt rose in waves, causing sweat to drip into her eyes.

She'd run a good way from the house before the sound of a UTV grew louder behind her. Crystal's head pounded. She'd had enough of him for one day.

Chapter Ten

The hot wind blew in Zach's face as he drove the side-by-side down the road.

Where was Crystal? He'd needed a minute in the barn to get his shit together before seeing her again at dinner, only she hadn't gone to the house.

Either Levi had picked her up, or she'd left by herself.

That woman was an endless disaster waiting to happen.

He'd almost kissed her in the barn. One second they'd been arguing, and the next she'd blurted out all that stuff about trying to protect him and teared all up.

She'd risked her reputation for him, or what she hoped to restore of it anyway, and that pissed him off. *He* was supposed to be the protector. All the sexual innuendo between her and Levi couldn't do her image any good. And damn that Levi. Maybe he hadn't wanted to do the scene, but nobody had begged him to flirt the way he did in the opening clip. He'd been infatuated with Crystal long before she ever set foot on the island. He had a mental little black book and Crystal might be the next entry on the mile-long contact list.

Zach's blood heated, and he tightened his grip on the steering wheel.

He'd swear he didn't have a green-eyed-monster bone in his body until she'd flirted with Levi and had made Zach's head explode. Somehow, she got to him.

He hadn't meant to squeeze her hand in the barn, but words wouldn't form. Next thing he'd known, they were inches apart, with his pulse racing and those sweet lips of hers so close he could almost taste them.

At least his mother's call from the deck had broken the spell. Then, he'd acted like an ass. He should have apologized on the spot, but his body had been revved up, and he'd felt like a teenage idiot with no control of his hormones. Control meant everything to him, and he'd lost it.

No excuse.

He was a grown man who'd been through a war and still couldn't figure out a way to squelch this stupid shit between him and Crystal.

He pressed the gas pedal, rounded a corner, and spotted her jogging on the side of the road. The tension in his shoulders eased.

Still, guilt sucker-punched him in the belly. She was running in the heat, with no ride back to the island, because of him. Running away from him. His ex-girlfriend had done the same. She couldn't handle his PTSD when he'd returned from Iraq. Not her fault. He never knew when an episode might happen, and they'd frightened her.

Him, too, at times.

That's why he needed his camp and safe place. Nature surrounding him kept the episodes at bay. Not the memories, but the incidents. No matter what, he was damaged goods. Yet, something about Crystal soothed him at the same time she ramped him up. The girl had spunk. He'd give her that. Still, even though she acted like she had it all together, she'd already messed up at the camp with the mudslide fiasco, and here she was again, doing something rash.

The temperature had hit a hundred, and she didn't even have any water. She could get heatstroke.

When he reached her, he slowed, matching her speed. "Get in, I'll drive you back."

She pumped her arms in rhythm with her feet and ignored him, facing forward.

"Please, let me give you a ride."

"Go away." She veered right and took off across a field.

He followed in the side-by-side as she glanced back and picked up the pace.

Without a doubt, the woman could run.

He frowned as she headed into the woods. His UTV wouldn't fit between trees. Damn it, this area wasn't part of the camp where he did regular rounds to check for hazards and dangerous wildlife. Crystal might step on a rattlesnake nest or trip a wire.

Zach's chest caved.

He slammed the brake and took a breath. No wires in the woods. No bombs. No triggers. No matter how many times he told himself it was in the past, memories overpowered logic.

Nothing to explode in the woods, but plenty of other dangers lurked, and Crystal wasn't paying attention right now. He had to make sure she didn't get hurt. He'd seen enough of that for one lifetime. He climbed out of the vehicle, jogged into the forest, and caught sight of her not far ahead.

The gurgling sound of rushing water filled the forest, and she halted by a river too wide to cross. Her shoulders rose and fell as she sucked in air.

Zach stopped a few feet behind her. "I need to talk to you."

She kept her back to him.

"First of all, you aren't being careful. Snakes curl up under fallen logs or sit in open spots of sunlight. You aren't wearing high boots and could be bitten by a poisonous one."

"Did you really chase me down to lecture me on my shoe selection again?" She continued to face the water and huffed.

He kicked a pinecone with his sneaker and sighed. "No. I wanted to apologize for what happened in the barn."

She turned around and crossed her arms. "Nothing happened as far as I'm concerned."

So that's the way she wanted to play it.

Denial.

Her pink cheeks glistened in the sun, and her damp shirt clung to her body. Even as a hot mess, she stirred his blood.

He shook his head and refocused. "If nothing happened, why are you running away?"

"I came with Levi. He had to go. You didn't want me there. End of story."

Shit. The hurt in her eyes cut right through him. "I never said that."

"Please, I'm not clueless." She walked to the edge of the water, scooped up a handful, and splashed her face.

Tiny rivulets trickled down her front. Zach's fingers itched to trace the trail. He fisted his hand and thumped it against his thigh.

Hard.

Wake up, asshole, and stop staring at her. So much for what he'd told himself about control. And despite what she'd said, Levi was into her. She could get hurt.

"You need to be careful about Levi." He picked up a curled caterpillar from the rocks and placed it in the grass.

"Back to this again?"

"I'm just trying to protect you." He straightened.

"I'm pretty sure he's not the brother I need protecting from."

Smart ass. She did have some comebacks, but he was too fired up to appreciate them.

"Levi shouldn't have left you at the house. My mother was worried about you. You didn't tell anyone you were leaving."

Crystal's nose wrinkled. "I never meant to upset her. I'm not used to...never mind." She thrust her shoulders back. "You should be thrilled I can't carry out my devious plot to play her."

He cocked his head. What was Crystal not used to? People being nice to her? The press had fawned over her forever.

He rubbed his temple. Regardless, he hadn't followed her to fight. "You aren't making it easy for me to apologize."

She tossed her hair back. "I don't want or need your apology."

The floral scent of her shampoo drifted past, teasing his nose. How could she smell so good after running in the heat? He cursed to himself. This was the shit that had gotten him into trouble at the barn.

"Well, I want to clear the air. I can admit when I've made a mistake. It won't happen again."

"A mistake?" She bristled.

"Yeah, I own up to my mistakes."

"Good to know." She dusted off her arm. "You might want to talk to a therapist because they can help people like you."

His body went rigid. How did she know about his PTSD? "People like me?"

"Yes. There's a psychological disorder where fans become obsessed with a celebrity and fantasize about them and sometimes even stalk them."

Relief flooded through him. She wasn't referring to his PTSD.

But then her snarky comment annoyed the shit out of him. He didn't follow Hollywood stars or care about their fake lives. He snorted. "You think I'm crazy and stalking you?"

"You did chase me into the woods, fanboy." She jutted out her chin.

"To apologize to you."

"For what? I told you nothing happened as far as I am concerned." She flicked a bug off her shirt. "And your obsession with me is referred to as being de-lu-sion-al."

More denial. His head reeled at the sing-song way she mocked him, dragging out the word. "Stop deflecting and pretending you don't know what I'm talking about. You were there, and it was real."

She shrugged. "Sorry. No idea."

"You're not getting off that easy. It wasn't just me."

He took a step forward, snagged her hand, and brought it to his chest. "This ring any bells?"

She caught her breath and gazed at his mouth.

His skin blazed where her soft hand rested. He couldn't stop his thumb from rubbing the side of her palm.

Her eyes widened, and the lines of her face softened.

She flattened her hand against his heart, raised her head, and parted her lips.

Busted.

The victory was short-lived because his body responded, and damn if he didn't want to wrap her in his arms and kiss that smart mouth of hers. Why on earth was he touching her?

Bad idea.

She exploded his senses, and she could deny the attraction all she wanted, but the pulse throbbing in her wrist? Not his imagination.

The last thing he needed to do was almost kiss her a *second* time.

Dumbass.

Let her think whatever she wanted. Talk about delusional, she owned the word. He tapped into his military training and flipped off all the breakers. Mission make-her-admit-it aborted. If she refused to accept his apology, he wouldn't beg. Guilt gone. He'd tried.

Taking a big step back, he let go of her hand.

Chapter Eleven

C rystal pushed off Zach's chest. Good God, she'd been leaning on him, almost begging to be kissed.

A second time.

Her cheeks stung, and she lowered her head. She didn't know what to make of her reaction. He'd proved his point. All he had to do was touch her, and she melted.

She had to keep her distance from him. "I'm done with your games. Leave me alone and don't follow me."

With hot tears burning her eyes, she took off running again. Every footstep freed her and annoyed her at the same time. She shouldn't have to deal with his antics. He'd apologized for almost kissing her and then tried to do it again. He toyed with her emotions and played her for a fool, having no idea about her past. She didn't have the experience or energy to deal with him.

Of course, she'd had her share of tabloid boyfriends for celebrity shots, but they'd meant nothing. The guys had no interest in getting to know her. Her only worth was a possible boost in their social media status. She'd never even had sex. It wasn't like she was saving herself, she'd just never wanted it. Her mother's revolving door of druggie boyfriends who had always tried to grope Crystal had turned her off. She'd put a deadbolt lock on her bedroom door and worn earbuds to drown out the sick, guttural noises coming from the next room.

She picked up her pace, pumped her arms, and burned the memories to bits. Somehow, she had to get through the next two months with Grizzly.

Sure, she'd been attracted to a few guys in the past. That was nothing compared to this crazy chemistry or whatever the hell she had for Zach.

She glanced back. He'd followed her out of the woods at a distance, and now sat on his stupid UTV.

Asshat better not make one move in her direction. Maybe he realized she was safely out of the dreaded forest and would leave her alone. Her parched throat begged for water, but she'd refused a ride from him. She'd rather deal with the heat and thirst. The crazy roller coaster of emotions he drew out of her, not so much.

She ran until a cramp formed in her side, forcing her to slow down. Finding a stump under the shade of a tree, she sat and tried to catch her breath. Too bad Jenna was off the grid. Crystal could use a friend to talk through everything. She plucked some leaves from a vine and tossed them as she waited for the cramp to subside.

After a few minutes, she felt better. She jogged the rest of the way to the park at a slower pace.

When she reached camp, she grabbed her canteen from the cement slab, where she'd moved some of her equipment, and sucked down the lukewarm water. Ugh, how she missed ice.

She fanned her face and frowned at the two tents pitched at the neighboring pad with an SUV parked in front. Someone had arrived and set up while she'd been gone. No one in sight, but they sure had a lot of stuff. Bikes, a canoe, life vests, pots, pans, bags of charcoal, and other junk littered the area. It looked like Outdoor World had puked next door. Who hauled around all that stuff and called camping a vacation?

"Murphy, stop!" A girl's voice rang out, and Crystal glanced down the hill.

She gasped as a fox ran out of her tent, chased by a big, yellow lab, that bounded past a teenager calling to him.

The fox dashed into the adjacent woods, and the dog followed at a dead run.

Her pulse jumped. She sprinted down the slope.

Good God. What chaos.

She opened the flap of her tent and gasped again. Muddy paw prints covered her sleeping bag and blanket. A candy bar wrapper, torn to pieces, littered the floor. Her head throbbed. All this over chocolate? She'd just gotten the place cleaned up from the flood, and now it was trashed again.

"Murphy." The girl's voice grew louder, and Crystal turned around to see the dog sprinting toward her. She jumped aside as the lab skidded to a halt in front of her and shook. Water flew off him, spraying her arms, face, and body. She gagged and ran a hand down her face. Bits of sand and clay flecked her shirt.

Tongue hanging out, the dog leaned against her and raised a paw.

Crystal had never been this close to a big dog, let alone one soaked in lake water. He didn't seem to want to bite her, but she couldn't be sure. She took a step back, her gut churning. This hound running loose around camp would be a nightmare. Only the way one ear flapped back and the other perked up kind of made him look harmless and cute, barring that he'd just shook water all over her.

The teenager, dressed in black leggings and a cropped tank that her bra showed through, caught up to them. She stopped, out of breath. Thick, black liner rimmed her brown eyes, and bright-blue eye shadow coated her lids. Heavy, dark blush plastered her cheeks. Crystal judged her to be about fourteen. She'd needed some help with makeup and clothing choices at that age too.

The girl pointed a finger at the dog while she sucked in air. "Bad boy, Murphy. Why did I get stuck watching you?"

The mutt licked her finger.

Crystal set a hand on her hip. "I take it this is your dog that wrecked my campsite?"

The girl's eyes widened, then slitted. "You're the celebrity my family had to sign a waiver for the privilege of camping next to. I should have known. You can't keep food in a tent, you know. This is your fault."

"I'm pretty sure dogs are supposed to be on leash here." She wasn't going to let this twit of a girl get under her skin. Let her act out with her parents.

A slim woman wearing jeans, a pink ballcap, and a white T-shirt appeared at the top of the slope. She called, "Murphy. Here, boy."

Murphy ran to her. The woman clipped a leash on his collar and walked him down to her tent. The girl continued to glare at Crystal.

Interesting. She had never had the chance to let her feelings show growing up. She always had to play the part, smile for the camera, not make any waves. At least this girl had pluck, albeit misdirected.

"Hi there, neighbor. I'm Mary. I hear you are some sort of star. I hope we don't disturb you. Looks like it's not off to a good start." The woman held a hand out to Crystal.

Some sort of star.

Crystal's stomach sank. Did no one know her anymore? Then again, this was a campground, and these people probably didn't watch much television.

She shook Mary's hand and quickly drew hers back. It was all too weird. She wasn't used to strangers touching her. Security used to keep people from getting too close.

"What happened, Angie? You know he has to be on leash here."

"Don't call me that. I go by Mallory now." The girl waved a hand at Crystal's tent. "Ask the diva. She left food out, and a fox came. Someone else can take care of Murphy. He's a pain in the butt."

"Angelica Romano, remember your manners. We're going to have words about this. You don't talk to people like that."

"Oh, a full name smackdown. Looking forward to it, *Mary*."
The girl spun on her heel and headed toward the slope.

Mary frowned. "I apologize for that. Let me see the carnage. I know this dog can do some damage."

Whoa. This woman had a lot on her plate dealing with that girl's attitude. "Don't worry about it. I'll figure it out."

"Nonsense. If my dog wreaked havoc, I'll fix it." She poked her head into Crystal's tent and sighed. "I'll clean this up. You need help moving your tent up to the slab?"

"No. That's not allowed."

"What do you mean that's not allowed?"

"I'm supposed to do everything on my own. That's what the show is about. Thanks for the offer, though," Crystal said.

"I feel terrible. I'm sorry about the mess."

A little boy yelled from the top of the hill. "Mom, we caught stripers. Two big ones."

Mary grinned. "Sounds like dinner for tonight. That's Johnny, my son. He's eight and is excited to catch fish. At some point, I'm sure you'll meet my husband, Paul. He'll be grilling it later. You should join us."

"Again, not allowed, but thanks."

She glanced at the tent that needed re-pitching and all the stuff she needed to move up the hill.

Dinner would have been nice since the fox had taken her candy bar, and she hadn't started a fire.

After watching another YouTube video, she managed to get the tent pitched on the cement slab. A spark of pride surged in her that she'd figured it out. Not easy. The clay soil was so hard it took some major effort to knock the stakes into the ground, but she was getting stronger in ways she couldn't at the gym.

Exhausted, she went to the bathrooms and took a shower. When she got back to her tent, she spied a box by the entrance with her name on it and the park office address. She hadn't ordered anything, though. The return label read, "Glamp Campers Boutique." Some place in California.

She took the package inside and opened the top. The box contained a pair of lightweight cargo pants, a long-sleeved, cream-colored shirt with wildflowers embroidered on the front, and a stylish pair of sunglasses. The multi-colored frame matched the shirt. She read the sticky note on top of a catalog.

We thought you might enjoy some more camp-suitable clothing. Compliments of our store. Maybe we could pay you in the future as an influencer if you make some posts that bring in business.

A ripple of pleasure passed through Crystal. They were giving her free clothes and offering a possible influencer job? Flipping through the catalogue, she found pictures of cute glamping attire. She bulked at the prices. Good thing they'd comped her the outfit. She changed into the clothes, put on the sunglasses, and stepped outside to take a selfie in front of her tent. She posted the shot and tagged the company. Smiling, she went back inside.

A sound came from her screened door like someone was flicking a finger against it. She slid open the zipper and the girl, Angie-who-insisted-on-being-called-Mallory, stood there with an attitude on her face. No other way to describe it.

The plate of food she held smelled amazing.

"This is from my mother. She said it's payment for the extra work Murphy caused." Angie thrusted the plate at Crystal and walked away, muttering, "I'm also supposed to apologize."

She smothered a laugh. Some apology. But it was nice there were people out there who still valued manners, like this poor girl's mother and Erin. Crystal opened the foil-covered plate of food, and her mouth watered. Baked beans, grilled fish, and a warm biscuit filled the paper plate. Even though she probably shouldn't have accepted it, she could argue that it was a fair trade. She'd thank Mary tomorrow.

Before heading to bed, she checked her notifications. Holy shit, she'd picked up a ton of followers, flooding her earlier post with comments. The boutique store had messaged a thank you and noted online sales were already coming in. Her belly did a happy dance.

Maybe she wouldn't need the stupid reality show to gain back her popularity. At the same time, she wouldn't have had the chance to promote the products if she wasn't on the island camping.

Her fingers itched. She glanced down. Little red bumps had appeared between them. Oh no, what was that about?

Chapter Twelve

Damn, her fingers itched. She rubbed them together and squinted at the growing rash. The bumps had spread up her arms. Maybe she should try to rinse them in the bathroom, although she'd already taken a shower. As soon as she finished eating, she'd head back there.

The food didn't disappoint. Crystal's tastebuds rejoiced, and she forced herself not to wolf down the dinner. She'd have to plan better. No one was going to feed her every meal. The producers had provided some sort of camper's packet meals that required boiling water. She'd have to start a fire.

More YouTube was needed. At least for tonight she had a full stomach. Granola and dried banana chips would be good enough for breakfast.

No doubt, Zach had a nice meal with his family and wouldn't miss a wink of sleep. He must be used to all the woodsy stuff. She couldn't be further out of her element. They had nothing in common, so Jenna's suggestion that Crystal should kiss him was nuts.

She shut down any thoughts of Grizzly. Right now, she had bigger problems. Maybe scrubbing her arms would help. She picked up her empty plate to put in the dumpster by the restroom. No more animal raids over trash or food in the tent. Who said she was a slow learner?

She dabbed a paper towel on her cheek and frowned at the red bumps. Great, the rash was spreading. She must have gotten something on her hands because that's where it started.

After washing her face and arms, she managed to get back into her tent without incident. She zipped the flap shut. Mission accomplished, only it was too warm inside. Even with the setting sun, the temps hadn't cooled. She opened the two screened windows and hoped for a cross breeze. What had she gotten herself into? Someone was sleeping comfortably in her air-conditioned penthouse.

The soft sound of guitar music floated in the wind along with the scent of burning wood. Who would make a fire when it was warm out? Crystal peered out the window at the neighbor's campsite. Sure enough, a small campfire crackled as Paul strummed a guitar. Mary sat in a chair next to him, stroking the big lab's head resting on her legs.

Johnny held a stick with marshmallows over the flames. "Why doesn't Angie sing anymore when you play, Dad? It used to be fun, all of us out here."

Paul's fingers faltered on the strings, and he gave a tiny shake of his head. "Not sure. I miss it too."

Mary placed a hand on his knee and waved at the stick. "Looks like those are about perfect, Johnny."

Crystal's heart ached as emotions flooded her. She'd never had a sibling or parents who cared about her.

"Angie, you want some marshmallows? They're ready," Johnny called out.

"It's Mallory, and leave me alone." The angry, muffled voice came from inside a tent.

Johnny's face fell, and Paul's face tensed, but he kept playing.

Mary got up and knelt by Johnny, patting his back. "They look great. I'd love one."

"Why does she hate me so much?" Johnny's lips trembled.

Crystal covered her mouth and fought back tears. She'd been that girl, mad at the world. Only, she'd never had a brother to take it out on. Poor boy.

"She doesn't hate you," Mary said. "She's just having a hard time right now. It's not you."

The dog came over to them, leaned against Mary, and licked the boy's hand.

"Uh oh, I think Murphy wants a marshmallow," Mary said.

The boy glanced down at him. "I know he can't have one, but we can roast a hot dog, right?"

Murphy barked, like he knew the word.

Johnny grinned and clapped his hands. "Hot dog, hot dog, hot dog. You want a hot dog?"

The mutt spun in a circle three times, chasing its tail, and flopped on the ground, tongue hanging out.

"Can you keep it down out there?" his sister yelled from the tent.

Paul put his guitar aside and stood. "I'll get the hot dog."

She backed up from the screen. It felt too much like spying. Sound carried in the woods and across the water. Paul's voice, controlled and quiet, mixed with the still-angry Mallory's, and then silence, until he came back out.

"Here ya go, son. One hot dog ready to be roasted."

"Thanks, Dad." The boy's defeated tone cut into Crystal.

She covered her head with the camp pillow and tried to stop the walk-down-memory-lane of her childhood. A tear slipped out of her eye anyway.

Enough.

The itching on her arms, hands, and face soon took over any thoughts. Thoughts of how she'd never been in school with friends. Thoughts of how she'd never been able to be herself. Thoughts of how she'd been used by her mother to make money to fuel her drug habit.

All ancient history, and nothing she could do to change it. Even buried deep after all these years, the bitter pain and anger still managed to surface.

The guitar music stopped and the woods quieted. Well, aside from the chirping crickets and croaking frogs. Not the worst sounds ever. It beat the sirens and booming rap music of the cars in the city.

Crystal tried not to scratch her arms. This would be a long night. She tossed and turned, unable to fall asleep.

By morning, her face had swelled to the point her skin hurt. The rash had spread to almost every part of her body. She slipped out of the tent and headed to the restroom for a look in the mirror. The dim, first rays of dawn lit the path.

She gasped at her reflection. Holy shit. Her face had swollen to double its normal size and her eyes were mere slits. The rest of her body hadn't fared any better. She could be cast as a sumo wrestler.

As much as she hated going to a doctor, she had no choice. She dialed Sydney's number. It went straight to voicemail, so she tried Trevor's, which did the same. Her gut twisted. They wouldn't be awake at six in the morning. She'd have to go to the villa and knock on their doors, but that was a two-mile walk. After splashing cold water on her face, she went back to her campsite.

She stuffed her water canteen into a small backpack with her credit cards and ID. Taking off on foot, she followed the road that led to the villas. She'd swear her face would explode if it got any tighter, and the itching had reached a frenzied point that made her want to roll her whole body on a steel wool pad.

If only she had another option. Without a doubt, Trevor would grab his camera and snap pictures of her. He'd find a way to leak some to the press under the guise of "marketing the show." She'd signed off on that as part of the contract. Her Pillsbury Doughboy, balloon-sized face would be splashed all over the tabloids. That was the last thing she needed to restore her image.

Two headlights appeared in the distance, accompanied by the low rumble of an engine. Seconds later, Zach's UTV came into sight.

Crystal's heart somersaulted and crashed. She sure as hell didn't want *him* to see her in this state. She stepped off the road and lowered her head, wishing she had a hat to hide her face. He glanced in her direction as he passed and kept going. She blew out a relieved breath, until she heard the beeping sound of him backing up.

Shit.

He stopped the vehicle in front of her, grabbed something from the back, and hopped out. Clicking on a flashlight, he shined it on her face.

For the love of God, why did this man always blind her? She tried to blink, the best she could, with a face swollen to the size of a jack-o'-lantern. "Can you please stop doing that?"

"No. I need more light to see what's wrong."

"It's none of your business. Just leave me alone." She stomped past him, but he caught up.

"Stop right now. This looks like a bad case of poison ivy, and you need to get to the doctor ASAP. You must be highly allergic to have this reaction."

No shit. She rubbed her arm, and he tapped it with the flashlight. "Don't do that, you'll make it worse. Where are you going?"

She patted her inflamed cheeks, which demanded scratching. "To the villas. I have to ask Sydney or Trevor to take me to a doctor. I'm not an idiot, you know."

"Why aren't they picking you up?"

"They're probably asleep. If you'd drive me up there, I'd appreciate it."

"Have you inhaled any smoke?"

"Yeah, from the campers next door."

Zach shook his head. "Okay, that's it. Get in. I'm taking you to Urgent Care. You might have breathed in some poison ivy from their fire, which could cause internal symptoms, affecting your respiration."

"The itching started before they made the fire."

"It might be a combination of contact with the plant and breathing it in since you don't know where they got the wood."

She swallowed. Her throat did feel scratchy.

"For once, can you just listen to me? This is a safety and health issue, which I can't have on my watch. Get in." He waved to the passenger seat of the UTV.

At this point, she really didn't want to deal with Trevor, so she climbed in. She dialed Sydney's number again and left a message. That would get her off Crystal's back if she bitched later about Zach's interference by taking her to the doctor.

Zach hit the accelerator. He pulled onto a dirt path and stopped in front of a small rancher in the woods. With a click, he unlocked a blue pickup truck in the driveway. He hopped out of the UTV and called over his shoulder. "Get in the truck. I'll grab you cold water from inside."

As she rounded the pickup, an army decal in the back window caught her eye, and she froze. Had Zach been in the military? Duh, the buzzcut and the drab, olive T-shirts, plus the confident way he handled everything at camp should have been dead giveaways.

Her heart rate ratcheted up. That comment she'd made when they first met about how he didn't know anything about danger must have insulted the hell out of him. No wonder he'd been dismissive and rude.

Gah. She'd been so self-absorbed and annoyed about being in the reality show that she'd missed all the signs. Jenna's father had been a SEAL, and Crystal knew how hard it was on him and the family when he was deployed. She had to apologize to Zach.

Chapter Thirteen

Zach snatched a water bottle from the fridge. He couldn't stay ahead of this train wreck of a woman. His plan, after yesterday's almost-kiss in the woods, was to avoid her as much as possible. He'd been building a mental wall between them and swore he wouldn't get close to her again. When he'd spied her walking down the road, he'd intended to drive right by until he'd seen her swollen face.

Flicking off the kitchen light, he headed outside. Crystal stood behind the pickup, staring at the rear window.

She glanced up at him.

"Why aren't you in the truck? We have to get going." He clicked the unlock button again.

"I...I need to ask you something."

"What?" He stopped in front of her.

She shifted her feet. "Were you in the army?"

That was a random question he wasn't expecting. "Yeah, why?"

"I didn't know that when I met you, and I want to apologize for that remark I made about danger. I'm sorry. I never meant to insult you. I have a lot of respect for those who serve." Her voice rang with sincerity and regret.

"Thanks for saying that. It's okay." He noted that her face was even more swollen, and concern knotted his stomach. "You aren't though, so let's go."

They got in the truck, and he backed out. He needed to keep her talking and hydrated.

"Take a sip of this." He handed her the bottle of cold water.

She didn't argue, taking a drink. That alone alarmed him. She never did what he asked.

"Do you know where and when you came in contact with the poison ivy plant?"

"Hmm." She strummed her fingers on the console, and his gaze dropped to her hand. He remembered the way her fingers had pressed against his chest, warming his skin. Even though she was a swollen, wretched mess, he responded to her. She made him *feel*. Something he couldn't afford to do. She'd be leaving, and he'd never see her again. Well, maybe splashed on a tabloid draped all over some movie star. He clenched his teeth.

Once again, he forced himself into mission-mode. He needed to get her to the clinic and shut down all his crazy reactions to her.

"Well, I did pick a couple of leaves off a vine when I was sitting under a tree yesterday."

This was better. Poison ivy discussions he could handle.

He told her to do a search for poison ivy plants on her phone. She did and frowned. "Yup, that's the plant I touched yesterday."

"I don't suppose you ever saw the pictures of poison oak and ivy in the safety manual I sent you?"

She didn't answer, which gave him the answer. Still, no sense rubbing it in. She was miserable and paying the price already.

"It's not too far. You okay?"

"Swell." Crystal shut her squinty eyes.

"That's an understatement."

She turned to him. "Was that a joke?"

"Maybe. I'm capable."

She huffed. "Could have fooled me."

Good. He had her attention, which meant she wasn't focusing on the rash, and as long as she talked, he'd know her throat hadn't closed up. "Well, you aren't exactly a barrel of laughs. What's the funniest thing you've ever done?"

"What?"

"I'm serious. Tell me."

Crystal shifted in the seat. "Once I put a rubber spider in my tutor's coffee cup."

"How did that work out?"

"Not well. She quit the next day."

Her voice sounded better. Zach kept his eyes on the road, hoping she'd keep talking. "So you got a new tutor?"

"Yeah, but she didn't last long. Not a fan of rubber spiders either."

He laughed, despite the situation. "That's all you've got? One trick?"

"Hey, why mess with success?" She shrugged. "What about you?"

"What about me?"

"Tell me something you did."

"I have two brothers. The list is long." Zach grinned.

Crystal's eyes widened.

"What are you looking at?"

"I just realized I don't think I've ever seen you smile."

He scrubbed a hand across his mouth. What did he say to that?

"You don't have to wipe it off your face and get all grumpy again. I'm just saying...never mind. Back to my question. Tell me something funny you did growing up."

Zach stopped at a light and tapped the steering wheel. "Levi used to eat cinnamon toast in the morning. I swapped it out for cayenne pepper."

"Oh no. That's mean."

"It was epic. He woke up fast that day. Only it backfired on me."

"How?"

"I forgot about it, and my mother made a coffee cake for a luncheon. I was grounded."

Crystal grinned, then winced.

"That hurt?"

"It's all right."

She pulled down the visor and checked her face in the mirror. "I'm a god-awful mess. I can't have people see me like this."

"No one's going to recognize you."

She glared at him. "That's not helpful."

"I'm not trying to be mean, but it's the truth. Your face is so swollen, you don't look like yourself. Hold on." He reached behind the seat to grab a hat. He handed it to her. "This might help. Keep it low over your eyes."

She snorted and pointed to the embroidered snake above the words "bite me" on the black cap. "You want me to wear this?"

"It's all I have. Take it or leave it."

He got out of the truck as she slipped the cap on, grumbling under her breath. He bit his cheek to keep from laughing. He'd achieved his mission, which was to keep her mind off things and get her to the doctor.

When they reached the door, she stopped. "You don't have to stay. I can call Sydney for a ride when I'm done."

He surveyed the parking lot. "Eh, there's hardly anyone here. It shouldn't take long to be seen. I'll wait."

As predicted, the place was empty except for one person ahead of Crystal. They sat in the far corner of the waiting room, and she kept her head down. It must suck to always have to worry about being recognized in public. He'd never given it much thought until now.

"How did you get started in the business? I know you were young."

Crystal's lips twisted. "My mother. She entered me in some baby photo contest, and I won. After that, I was her ticket."

"What do you mean?"

She shrugged. "She came to Hollywood to be an actress and never made it. Once she realized she could market me, that's all she cared about. She controlled all the money and used it however she wanted."

Her bitter tone wasn't lost on Zach. Her mother had "marketed" Crystal? Didn't sound like much love in that. "Do you mean she bought a bunch of pricey stuff?"

Crystal gazed out the window. "If only. Suffice it to say she had an expensive habit."

Shit. So she was a user in more ways than one. "What about your father? What did he do?"

"No idea. I never met him and don't even know his last name. My mother changed mine to Lovechild when I was a kid so I'd have a Hollywood name." Crystal rolled her eyes.

A door opened to the waiting room, and a nurse called for Crystal. She picked up her purse and followed the nurse.

He sighed and sat back. A fist squeezed his heart as he pictured a little girl with no father and a druggie mother. If Crystal tried to scare her tutors, she couldn't have been close to them. She must have no idea what it was like to have a family. Sure, he and his brothers fought all the time growing up, and still did, but when push came to shove, they'd go to the mat for each other.

Damn it.

He wanted to keep Crystal at arm's length and continue thinking of her as an entitled star. Hard to do now with what he knew. She'd just put a crack in the mental wall he'd constructed, sharing some of her painful past. No wonder she'd gotten angry at him for accusing her of playing his mother. Sounded like she'd never had a real mom.

He puffed out a breath, and a few minutes later Crystal came out of the back, holding paperwork. Again, she kept her head down, even though only one person sat in the waiting room. He followed her to the door and outside.

"What did the doctor say?"

Crystal muttered as she climbed into the truck, "Poison ivy. I got a shot, and he called in a prescription for a cream."

"To the pharmacy next door?"

She jerked her head in a nod, took off the hat, and faced the passenger window.

"They aren't open yet. I'll come back at nine to get them for you."

"Thanks, but you've done enough. I'll figure it out."

Something was wrong. She hadn't even glanced in his direction. "Crystal?"

"Hmm?"

"What's up? Look at me."

She continued to face the window.

Maybe the doctor had scared her, or someone had recognized her in the back and embarrassed her. "Okay, we're not leaving until you tell me what's wrong."

She finally turned to him. "I appreciate you bringing me here, but please, just take me back." Her voice quivered.

What had happened?

Chapter Fourteen

Crystal's hands shook, so she flattened them on her pants. The talk about her doped-up mother had brought back pain. When the doctor had picked up a needle, she'd flashed back to the days when used syringes littered their home. Her gut coiled at the memory of wearing too-large rubber gloves to toss them out before her mother and the boyfriend-of-the-day emerged from the bedroom.

And like a vulnerable teenager, Crystal had blabbed about her past to Zach. What had gotten into her? The last thing she wanted was for him to feel sorry for her. She didn't talk about her mother to anyone except Jenna, and only on rare occasions. Crystal had worked hard to hide her mother from public view.

She'd let her guard down with Zach after he'd been so nice to her, making her laugh about the pranks. When he'd smiled, his entire face lit up and had taken her breath away.

She knew he'd kept her talking to keep her mind off the intense itching. It worked. But now the shame and humiliation of what she'd blurted out bubbled up like an Alka-Seltzer in a champagne flute.

Whatever attraction they'd shared had to be over, at least for him. He'd never look at her the same way after seeing her in this condition. She'd learned long ago beauty was the allure. Her heart sank into her itchy feet. She should be relieved. Those almost kisses wouldn't happen again. Fine by her.

Only it wasn't.

She glued her face to the passenger window. He didn't ask any more questions, and she welcomed the silence. She might choke up again if she had to talk. Too many hurtful memories swirled in her head.

Some of the terrible itching had ceased since the shot. She touched her face, which had cooled a bit.

Ugh. She'd have to deal with Sydney and Trevor once she got back to the campsite. The doctor had gone over care instructions with her, which included keeping cool, taking tepid baths, staying out of the sun, and applying chilled compresses. None of that could happen in a tent with hundred-degree temps and no air conditioning.

When they arrived at her campsite, Trevor had his camera aimed in her direction, with Sydney standing beside him. Crystal had texted her from the doctor's office to let her know they were headed back. So far, the only shots they'd have of her would be from the stationary cams, and she doubted in the dim light they showed much of her face.

Her muscles tensed. Trevor would try to take close-up pictures for sure. As much as it killed her, she grabbed the snake hat from the console. "Can I please borrow this?"

"Knock yourself out."

She thrust the hat low on her head, got out of the truck, and approached Sydney. "I'd appreciate if we stopped filming for a few days."

Sydney sneered. "I don't think so. We're on a schedule."

Not even ten in the morning, and the heat and humidity had built. Crystal swiped sweat from the side of her face. The sun shining on her arms aggravated her rash.

"Take off the hat," Trevor said.

Crystal shook her head. "No. I can't be exposed to the sun."

"Excuse me. I think you might want to look at these instructions from the urgent care." Zach handed the release papers from the visit to Sydney, who scanned them and frowned.

Crystal stole a glance in his direction. Arms crossed and legs planted wide, he stood firm. "I'm responsible for the safety of the campers, and she can't follow the doctor's instructions in this environment."

Sydney passed the papers to Trevor, who lowered the camera. "What do we do?"

The longer Crystal stood in the sun, the more she itched. She had to figure out where to go and get out of the heat. "Can I stay in a villa or cabin for a few days?"

"Sorry, all booked," Zach said.

Crystal turned to Sydney. "Can I share your villa? I have a sleeping bag and don't need a bed."

Sydney cringed and took a step back. "No way. I don't want to be anywhere near you and get that shit."

Of course, Sydney had no feelings or filters. Crystal had one more suggestion. "How about a nearby hotel?"

"It's not in the budget." Sydney pointed to Zach. "You're insisting on her staying somewhere else. What about your place?"

Zach shook his head. "It's small. One bedroom."

Crystal held up her hands. "Well, I'm out of ideas."

Sydney looked at Trevor, who shrugged. "What about Levi? She could stay with him."

"Now you're talking." Sydney nodded. "We need to get him back in the picture anyway."

"No," Zach said, an edge to his voice. "He lives on a small houseboat, also one bedroom."

Sydney smirked. "That's even better."

Zach's nostrils flared, and his lips thinned. His phone rang, and he glanced at the screen. "I have to take this." He walked back to his truck.

Crystal couldn't blame him. Not his problem where she ended up. She stepped under the shade of a tree and tried not to scratch her arms. "I refuse to invade Levi's space, and we aren't sleeping together. I won't pretend otherwise."

"This show needs some spice, so you *will* continue to at least flirt with him. It's part of the script now. Don't go anywhere. I need to talk to Trevor." Sydney walked over to him.

A dog barked, and Johnny bounded down the slope, dragged by Murphy like a water skier hanging onto the leash. The dog slid to a stop in front of Crystal and yet again shook lake water on her. He leaned against her and raised a paw a second time.

Crystal shuddered. Did this mutt live in the lake?

"Sorry, lady. He's strong." Johnny's eyes bugged out. "Whoa. Are you okay? Your face is huge."

Crystal wiped some mud off her arm. Children spoke the truth. "Yeah, I'm kind of a mess."

"Eh, no worse than my friend after he stepped on a wasp's nest." Johnny shrugged.

Crystal's heart tugged. This boy didn't see her as hideous like the rest of the world would.

Angie-Mallory yelled from their camp, "Johnny, get back here. Dad said to leave the diva alone."

Johnny rubbed the dog's head. "I don't know what a diva is, but if Murphy likes you, so do I."

The mutt barked. Johnny laughed and raced him to their campsite.

Crystal shut her eyes. Dogs and kids saw people beyond physical appearances.

Sydney came back at the same time Zach approached and said, "I changed my mind. She can stay at my place."

Chapter Fifteen

Crystal packed a bag of clothes and essential toiletries while Zach went to the pharmacy. Sydney had accepted his offer to pick up Crystal's prescription. Like Sydney had anything better to do with the film on hold. Lazy jerk.

Guilt weighed down on her shoulders. He'd done enough and had a camp to run. When Sydney had asked why he changed his mind, he'd grumbled something about Levi. Why would he even care if Crystal stayed at Levi's, not that she'd consider it?

Zach said there was only one bedroom in his house. How would they manage the space? They'd be elbow to elbow in that place. Maybe the poison ivy was messing with her brain because a thrill ran up her spine at the thought. She'd probably end up crashing on a couch, which was still a step up from the concrete slab.

His voice sounded outside of the tent. "Here when you're ready."

Her stomach fluttered. Okay. She was going to do this. Stay at his place with him. She unzipped the tent flap and stepped outside, carrying her suitcase.

He picked up a duffle bag and tossed it inside her tent. "Got what you need?"

Crystal blinked. "What's that bag for?"

"We're swapping. I'll camp here until you're cleared to be outside again."

Her heart sank along with unfounded hope. What else had she expected? Of course, he didn't want to stay with her. Just because he'd been kind to her at the doctor's office didn't change anything.

"Is there a problem?" he asked.

"No. I didn't realize...I mean, I thought..."

He cocked his head. "Look, all I'm doing is trying to help you out here. There's not enough room for both of us at my place."

"Oh, I know." She waved a hand. "I wasn't sure where you were going to stay is all. I thought maybe your mom's." The lie slid off her tongue. She had to save face somehow.

"No. I need to be on location, and we don't have any other vacant campsites."

"I appreciate you giving up your house for me." She bent and busied herself fussing with the clips on her suitcase. Not that they needed any adjustments.

"Your face looks redder. Are you feeling any more swollen?"

"I'm fine. Just hot."

"It's been a long morning. I have your cream. Let's get you back to my place, where it's cool."

"Thank you. I'm sorry for being grumpy. I'm grateful for all your help."

"It's okay. You've been through a lot. Rest tonight, and I'm sure you'll feel better soon," he said.

She must have drifted off during the short ride to his home because he gently shook her. "We're here."

"Great." She rubbed her eyes and got out of the truck as he grabbed her suitcase.

When they entered, he flicked on the lights. "It's a small place."

He wasn't kidding. The tiny kitchen had a counter between the eating area and family room. Not much furniture. A wooden table with four chairs, a loveseat, and a TV on a nightstand filled the sparce space.

Cold air blew from a window AC unit, and Crystal ran to it and put her face in front of the vents. "This feels so good."

"Yeah. Staying cool should help your condition. That has a thermostat. Adjust it how you want, and the fan in the hall will blow air into the bedroom." He pointed down the hallway. "That's straight ahead, bathroom on the right. I'll leave this cream on the table. You need anything before I go?"

He seemed like he couldn't get out of there fast enough. Looking at her had to be a hardship. "No, thanks. You've done more than enough already."

"All right, then." He reached for the door and paused. "Just to warn you, my mother might stop by. She has a habit of doing that."

"No problem. Should I text you if she does?"

"Nah. She has radar or something because she always finds me and my brothers." He shook his head and shrugged as if embarrassed.

Crystal smiled. No hiding from Mom. And that thought sank her spirits. She had plenty of experience in that department.

Zach left, and she dragged her suitcase to the bedroom. *His* bedroom. His unique scent of musk and pine lingered in the room. She'd be breathing that in all night. The intimacy of sleeping in his bed made her shiver, and she turned her attention to something more neutral.

Bookshelves above the cherry wood dresser held hardbacks for the most part, history and war related. Fiction and nonfiction. Made sense given his military service.

Among the books was a leather photo album. Was it nosy to look inside? Maybe it would give her some insight on Zach, because the man was locked up tighter than Fort Knox.

She slid the book off the shelf and sat on the edge of the bed. When she opened the first page, she grinned at the pictures. Zach had to be about seven in the first one. He and his brothers aimed squirt guns at each other, their swim trunks dripping wet. As she flipped through the book, the boys grew older, but Zach always had a face-splitting grin. She paused at a shot of him smeared with mud, standing next to a man who might be his father, given the age and resemblance.

Zach gazed up at the man, whose hand lay on Zach's head like he'd been tousling his hair. Crystal's eyes watered. Whoever had taken the picture had captured the pure love between the two. A gentle smile curved the man's mouth, and laugh lines spread from the corner of his eyes. Zach's face beamed with adoration.

No one had ever looked at Crystal that way. Hell, she'd never even met her father. She swallowed and flipped another page.

Near the end of the book, she stopped at an image of him on the tarmac, dressed in a camouflage uniform, his arm around an attractive brunette. Her head rested against his shoulder, and she bore a faint, somber smile. Had to be a girlfriend.

A pang of jealousy ran through Crystal. It appeared this woman was no longer with Zach, but what had she lost, and did he have regrets?

Crystal shook her head. They might have had a happy life together. She turned the last page. It held a picture of someone pinning a medal onto Zach's uniform.

With a sigh, she shut the book and placed it back on the shelf.

She had more questions than answers now about Zach. One thing was for sure, he'd grown up loved.

Someone knocked on the door, and Crystal went to answer it. Erin stood on the stoop holding a vase with roses.

"Oh my goodness. That is a bad case of poison ivy. You poor thing." She handed the flowers to Crystal. "Zach mentioned you were staying here, and I thought these might brighten up the place. He's not much on decorating. I picked them fresh from my bushes."

Crystal's heart lifted at the unexpected kindness. "Thank you. This is so sweet."

"Are you feeling okay?"

She nodded. "Much better since the shot and the cream."

"The boys had this many times growing up. You'll be fine. It takes a few days, though. Hang in there. I didn't see Zach's UTV. He's not here?"

"No. He left a little while ago and is going to stay at my camp until I'm better."

"Not a problem. I'll find him."

Without a doubt. Crystal grinned and opened the door wider. "Would you like to come in?"

"Sure, but I have to grab the casserole first." Erin turned and headed toward her car.

Casserole?

Erin bustled inside, carrying the dish. "I bring the guys a meal every week. Can't rely on them to cook for themselves. Not healthy, anyway."

She set the baking pan on the counter, then glanced up and gasped. "Whoa. I can't believe my eyes."

"What? Is something wrong?"

Bringing a hand to her chest, she crossed the room and stood in front of the AC unit. "I thought it felt cooler in here. Alert the presses. I can't believe Zach bought an air conditioner."

"Wait. This is new?" Crystal bit her lip. No way. Please, no way, no way, no way. She couldn't stand the thought that he'd spent money and installed it just for her.

"Do you know how long I've been trying to get him to buy one of these? This place is hot as the blazes in the summer, and he's always refused. Until now."

"I don't know what to say. I've never even been here. I assure you—"

"Relax." Erin laughed. "It's the best ever. He wouldn't get it for himself."

"I promise I'll pay him for this as soon as I can." Humiliation washed over Crystal. Her face might never cool down.

"Don't you dare." Erin strode to Crystal and touched her shoulder. "He'll get paid back. I never used to stay here long because of the heat. Now I can visit longer."

"I'm sure he'll be happy about that."

"He'd never admit it." A mischievous smile lit Erin's face. "You, my dear, are special. I never saw this coming, but it explains why he's been grumpier than usual."

Crystal frowned. "I seem to put him in a bad mood."

"It's temporary. Trust me. He's just figuring things out."

Erin hummed as she went back into the kitchen. She pulled the foil off the casserole. "This is vegetable lasagna made from my garden. Make sure you have some. Can't be cooking when you're all hot and swollen." She pointed to a loaf of bread next to a toaster oven. "I baked that yesterday. Help yourself."

A lump formed in Crystal's throat. This woman was so caring and kind. She'd just met Crystal and was treating her like family. And how nice it must be to have someone bring over homemade meals and fresh-baked bread every week. Did Levi, Brody, and Zach have any idea how lucky they were?

"Oh, I almost forgot to tell you." Erin held up a finger. "I looked into using the farm as a wedding venue, and you're right. It's trending, and there's real money to be made. I sure wish I could hire you to do the marketing and decor."

"Thanks. I'd love that kind of job. But—"

"I know you won't be here. I appreciate you giving me this idea. I'll figure something out."

Erin's phone rang. "Hmm. I better answer this. Excuse me." She walked down the hallway.

Crystal couldn't help but overhear her in the small quarters.

"Oh, well...yes...of course. I mean, I understand. Yes, I still want you to come. This weekend will be f-fine," Erin said in a shaky voice.

Crystal cocked her head and grimaced.

Erin sounded stressed. Who had she been talking to?

Chapter Sixteen

Z ach swung by the park office and hopped out of the UTV.

He'd passed Sydney and Trevor, who stood talking on the side of the building, out of sight now. He paused at the sound of their voices coming from around the corner.

"We're really getting behind, and now she's not even on the set," Sydney said.

"It's not as bad as you think. Don't forget we have all those earlier scenes. Why does Crystal keep saying she won't approve certain shots?" Trevor asked.

"Apparently, she thinks she has a say, and I'm not telling her otherwise or she might stop doing dumb stuff. That's what people want to see. It's on her if she didn't read the contract."

A wave of shock ripped through Zach's body. Holy shit. The production company planned to show all those humiliating scenes Crystal said she'd never authorize. Hadn't her agent explained this to her?

Considering she'd shoved his safety manual back at him, saying it was too long, she probably hadn't read the contract either.

The tips of his ears turned hot. He had to warn her. Maybe there was something she could do about it.

Brody came out of the building, frowned at a pile of boxes, and shook his head. Did the guy ever *not* have a scowl on his face?

"What's going on?" asked Zach.

Brody waved at the stack. "These are all addressed to Crystal. You need to take them to her, because I don't have room. Levi already dropped something off yesterday for her."

Zach frowned. Why on earth would she order so much stuff when living in a tent?

Irritation crept up his spine.

Of course, she wouldn't know how to be a minimalist. She had no place to keep all the crap, either. He'd have a word with her because he sure as shit wouldn't be the campground delivery service.

"Sydney paid me a visit, and she's not too happy." Brody picked up a box and took it to the UTV. "She said you keep interfering, and it's causing production delays and loss of footage. They're threatening to withhold money to offset their costs. What the hell are you doing at the camp?"

Zach hoisted another box onto the pile. "Crystal is a hazard to herself. I'm trying to keep her safe."

"Well, what's she doing at your place? Sydney was pissed that Crystal is offsite. It shuts production down until she's back."

As always, Brody's questions got under Zach's skin. "They didn't have any cool place for her to stay. She's under doctor's orders, so I worked something out. It's not costing them anything."

"That's not true. It's wasted time, and they're paying for accommodations while no work is done. You need to stay out of the way."

Typical Brody, dishing out orders. Zach's temper flared, and his face burned. "I voted against having them here. I knew there'd be problems, but you and Levi don't have to deal with them. You need to stay out of my business because the camp is my territory."

"Well, we can't afford to be in breach of contract, so knock off all this superhero shit and let them finish already."

"Superhero shit? What's that supposed to mean?" Zach narrowed his eyes.

"You tell me. I've never seen you act like this with any other camper."

Levi came around the corner of the building. "Do I need to put you two in time-out? What are you arguing about now?"

"Nothing." Brody and Zach said at the same time.

Levi smirked. "Right." He glanced at the boxes piled up on the UTV. "Are these for Crystal?"

"Yeah, and Zach, tell her we're going to start refusing packages unless she figures out a way to get them herself and store them. This wasn't part of the deal," Brody said.

"Fine by me." Zach climbed into the vehicle, started it, and pulled out, revving the engine. Damn that Brody. Superhero shit? What a crock.

But was it? Maybe Brody's shot had hit a little too close to the bullseye. Zach did feel the need to protect Crystal, and he'd never hosted any other campers at his home.

The warm wind fueled the frustration burning inside. Everything about this reality show had been nothing but problems. Crystal was a hot mess with no idea what she was doing, and now she was staying at his house and racking up inventory.

He pulled into his driveway. Carrying two boxes, he pushed open the door and deposited them on the floor. He still fumed about the stupid deliveries and even more about being called out by Brody.

Crystal came out from the kitchen. "Your mom was here. She left to take casseroles to Levi and Brody. I didn't expect to see you so soon, but I'm glad you stopped by because we need to talk about this air conditioner you just bought."

"Why? Is it not working?" The room felt cool.

"It's fine, but I feel terrible that you got it for me. I'm going to pay you back for it. I mean—"

"Don't worry about it." He held up a hand. "We have bigger fish to fry right now."

She blinked. "Like what?"

"All these boxes." He tapped one with his shoe.

She shrugged. "They're your packages. Put them wherever you want."

"Not mine, *yours*. And there's more." He went back outside, grabbed the other cartons, and plopped them next to the first pile.

Crystal's eyes popped wide and she bent, reading the labels. "I didn't buy anything. I have no idea why I'm getting deliveries."

"They have your name on them. I'm sure you're used to ordering all kinds of things out there in Hollywood, but this is a campground. Brody said he's going to refuse deliveries if you don't make arrangements to get them. There's no space for—"

"I know there's no room for these. I'm telling you, I didn't order anything." Her brow wrinkled. "Hmm...companies must be sending me merchandise now to market, I guess."

"To market?" What was she talking about?

Crystal shrugged. "I've been posting pictures and my followers are picking up. Have you seen my social media numbers?"

His brain hurt. "No. I don't have any accounts. I run a campground, remember? And did the production company even give you permission to do this?"

"Yes. Sydney seems excited it will bring more attention to the show. I think I might be on my way to becoming an influencer."

"An influencer?"

Crystal nodded. "Yes, it's someone who promotes products, and their followers buy them. I'm helping businesses."

"Virtuous." Zach rubbed his forehead. He had no idea what to make of someone being an "influencer." His exasperation over the whole situation reached its limit.

"Don't diss it. The results have been good. Now, we really need to talk about this air conditioner."

"No, we don't. You aren't paying me for it. I bought it for the house."

"But you wouldn't have if I wasn't here."

"I'm not going to argue with you. The subject is closed." If he didn't step outside, his head would explode. "I need to check on some things. I'll be back."

He jogged down the front porch steps and headed to the woods. He stopped, ran a hand down his face, and sucked in the sweet scent of wildflowers. This he could relate to.

Influencers, not so much. Why did people need other people to tell them what to buy? Her world made no sense. And how did Crystal know the window unit was new? He grunted. That's right. His mother had been there. Of course, she must have told Crystal. Those two were getting way too chatty. No way he'd take any money for it. Crystal would only be there for a couple of days.

He hiked for a bit, and as always, nature calmed his frayed nerves.

On the walk back to the house, the conversation he'd overheard between Sydney and Trevor kept echoing in his head. That was more important than the packages and the influencer shit. He had to tell Crystal. She wasn't going to like hearing it, but she needed to know.

He entered to find Crystal strolling across the family room in hiking boots, staring down at her feet.

"These are a little big. I think they'll work if I wear an extra pair of socks, though. They feel amazing."

Zach glanced at the high-end boots. No kidding. They should, for what they cost. He recognized the brand and knew the value of paying for decent gear. But she was in this for the short term, not ten years. His gaze traveled along her toned legs as she circled the room. Her sassy strut and the delight in her eyes made his blood warm. Damn it. He responded to her even when he was annoyed.

All sorts of paraphernalia cluttered the kitchen table. Hats with ribbons around them, patterned socks, some sort of shawl, and various bottles that might be mosquito repellant.

"I called Sydney while you were gone. Tell Brody she'll pick up any deliveries and keep them at the villa." Crystal shrugged. "I mean, she's going to actually keep them. It's the deal we made. I can use the products for my posts, but she'll own them afterwards."

Zach cocked his head. "That doesn't seem fair."

"Eh, increasing my following is what's important, and making some money from my influencer posts, not the actual stuff."

He hadn't expected that comment. She seemed so into the products. Wasn't she all about the material world?

She sat and unlaced a boot.

"Listen, there's something I need to tell you."" He leaned against the counter.

"What?"

"It's about the show. I don't think these producers have your best interests in mind. They—"

"Oh, I know. All they care about are ratings." She waved a dismissive hand. "Don't worry. I'm used to this business."

"I'm not sure you understand. They—"

"Believe me. I've been doing this all my life. There's nothing you can tell me that I don't already know." She yanked the boot off and placed it back in the box. "These really are nice."

Aggravation pricked his chest. She had no right to blow him off and talk down to him.

Erin stuck her head in the doorway. "Zach, I have a problem. Can I come in?"

He tensed. "Sure. What's wrong?"

She entered and frowned. "My friends Nancy and Harvey are coming sooner than expected. This weekend, in fact, and your old room isn't ready."

"That's the problem?"

He heaved a sigh of relief, forcing himself to remember problems to civilians were not the same as problems on deployment.

His mother wrung her hands. "I know you'd planned to repaint it next month, but now it can't wait. I haven't even had a chance to pick out the decor."

Crystal paused from unlacing her other boot. "I'd be happy to help. I have a knack for designing. The stores are all air-conditioned, so I could help you shop. I might as well do something useful."

"Everybody hold on a second. I need to think." Zach pressed his fingers to the bridge of his nose. He took a deep breath. "It's Tuesday, and they're coming when?"

"Saturday," his mom said.

"That doesn't give us much time. I'll have to juggle things at the camp."

"Like I said, I'm happy to help." Crystal pulled off the boot. "I love to paint. After we shop, we can hit up the hardware store for supplies."

"Wait. *You* love to paint?" Zach pointed a finger at Crystal.

"Yup. It's all settled. My way of paying you both back for the food and hospitality."

The last thing Zach needed was to be holed up in a tiny space with Crystal. That went against his plan to avoid her. "Thanks, but I can do it myself."

His mother took a step toward him. "The job will go faster with two of you working, and I don't want to keep you from the camp longer than necessary."

Her anxious eyes squashed his heart. He did have a large group of Boy Scouts coming on Friday. If he knocked the project out in two days, it would be helpful. "All right. We'll need to get started tonight."

"Perfect. This will give me something to do. It's a win-win-win." Crystal picked up a hat from the table and perched it on her head. "What do you think, Erin?"

"Adorable."

"As soon as my face clears, I'll post a picture wearing this. You like it, Zach?" She brushed back her hair on one side, her eyes sparkling. Her innocent playfulness reminded him of what he could never be to her or anyone. He'd lost that side of himself overseas. All the more reason to limit their time together. She'd go back to Hollywood and find some fun guy who'd make her happy.

"It's nice," he managed to choke out.

"Don't let us hold you up, Zach. I'm sure you have things to do." His mom rested a hand on Crystal's shoulder. "Looks like us girls are going shopping. We can stop by the house so I can show you the room first."

Zach's stomach clenched. They were getting too cozy. Walking hand in hand to the barn, now shopping and decorating together. Both of them could get hurt. When his girlfriend had broken up with him, his mom had taken it hard. She didn't need to get attached to another woman who would soon walk out of their lives.

He shook his head. "Never mind. This isn't going to work."

Chapter Seventeen

"We talked this all through. What's the problem with me helping to paint the room?" Crystal gathered up her hair and stood in front of the window unit, letting the cool air blow on her itchy skin.

"I don't think us working together is a good idea." Zach's gaze locked on her eyes.

She caught her breath at the intensity. Why was he looking at her like that?

"Why?" Crystal asked.

"I really don't have time to talk about this. Let's move on." He dug his keys out of a pocket.

Erin glanced between the two of them and plucked up her cell phone, a ghost of a smile tugging at the corners of her mouth. "I'm sorry, Zach. I don't mean to put so much pressure on you. Let me give Levi a call and see if he can—"

"No. He's busy," Zach said in a gruff tone.

Crystal winced. She didn't want Levi dragged into this now.

Erin said, "Well, so are you, honey. I'll check and see—"

"Don't bother. I got this." Zach placed a hand over Erin's and pressed the phone down.

"Not without help. If you're too uncomfortable working with Crystal, I'm sure Levi can. They seem to get along splendidly."

Zach's nostrils flared. "I never said I was uncomfortable. I said it wasn't a good idea."

Erin gestured to Crystal. "She's very pretty. You can't help it if you feel uncomfortable working with her. I'll make other arrangements."

A flush of heat rose to Crystal's face. She was anything but attractive with bumpy rashes everywhere. Why on earth would Erin say she was pretty?

"I'm not uncomfortable with...with anything," Zach grated out.

"It's okay. I understand." Crystal let go of her hair, shaking it down in an attempt to cover her face as she lowered her head. Of course, he wouldn't want to be stuck in a room looking at her hideous condition. Maybe she could find a way to help without forcing him to be disgusted, sharing space with her.

The silence was deafening.

Crystal shuffled her bare feet, staring down at them.

"I'm done with this conversation." Zach trudged to the door.

"Does that mean you'll let her help?" Erin asked.

"Yeah. Just leave Levi out of this. I'll be back later to pick you up, Crystal." He opened the porch door.

Erin grabbed her purse. "No need. We'll do our shopping, and she can have dinner with me at the house, if that's okay with Crystal?"

"Sure. I appreciate the invite." It would save her an extra car ride with Zach, who was in a rush to get away from her.

"All right. I'll be over later." Zach left and shut the door behind him.

Crystal mentally ticked through her inventory of clothes. She had a long sleeve shirt, pants, and a hat. He wouldn't have to see much of her body at all. She could do this. She could still help. She could turn the room into something beautiful that would make Erin proud to host her friends. The woman deserved it, as nice as she was being to Crystal.

It had been a while since Crystal had sketched and painted. She'd needed an outlet as a teen, alone in her room at night with the door deadbolted to keep out her mother's boyfriends. Painting had become her hobby. That led to marketing and design. Like a sponge, she'd soaked it all up. Excitement bubbled and tickled her ribs at the chance to use her creative skills again.

Crystal considered the timeframe. The room wouldn't be ready for detailing until the paint dried. She'd need to come back to finish Friday night because she might be on the set again during the day. Zach would be busy with the scouts, and she didn't want him driving her anyway. She nibbled her lip as a plan formed. When she had time, she'd give Levi a call.

"Are you okay?" Erin asked.

"Yeah, but I do have a confession."

"What?"

She shrugged. "I have painted before, but never a room."

Chapter Eighteen

Zach tossed supplies into the back of the UTV. He'd rushed through his park rounds to make time for painting. If they got the primer on tonight, he could finish two coats by Friday.

He frowned. What had gotten into his mom with her weird comments earlier, and why had she kept saying he was uncomfortable?

His palms sweated. The situation had gotten weirder and weirder to the point he'd had no words and left before he imploded. And why did everyone keep bringing Levi into the equation? Maybe there was something going on between him and Crystal. Zach's gut roiled.

He climbed into the UTV and started the engine. How Crystal "loved to paint" was beyond him. He doubted celebrities dirtied their hands. They hired people to do manual labor. Who knew?

If all went well, they'd slap up the primer and be out of there.

Yet, the image of Crystal's blotchy face, with that hat tilted on her head, popped into his mind. The rash took nothing away from her shining eyes. She'd seemed to have let go with no cameras filming her. A playful, fun side of her had come out without the worry of her image. She'd never looked more beautiful. His heart had warmed, right before it had crashed with the reality that he'd never share such free-spirited feelings.

He could picture some guy snatching the hat from her head and running off with it. She'd give chase. They'd laugh and crash into each other and end up kissing.

Zach's lungs deflated. What was wrong with him? That's exactly what Crystal needed. Not some ticking timebomb of a person who might go off at any moment and scare her to death.

Soon enough, she'd be back in Hollywood. He shouldn't even be thinking about her. Right now, he had a task to complete, which was all that mattered. Although it bothered him that Crystal had shut him down when he'd try to warn her about the contract. He was still pissed at the way she'd dissed him. But she needed to know. Maybe when he cooled off, he'd try to talk to her again.

He pulled into his mom's driveway, parked next to Brody's car, and hauled the supplies he'd brought up the porch steps.

His mother opened the screen door. "Hi, hon."

"What's Brody doing here?" Zach asked.

"He's not. Levi borrowed his car because his motorcycle is in the shop. He's fixing the fence to keep the rabbits out of my garden, then he's going to mow the lawn."

"That's good." It helped that both of his brothers pitched in to keep up with repairs and chores.

"Crystal is upstairs. She found a ladder to use and is putting up blue tape. Oh, and Levi offered to take her back to your place when he's done if she's tired and wants a ride."

Zach's blood heated. "I bet he did."

"He's just being nice. She's had a long day and was super helpful. I can't wait to see how the room turns out." His mom smiled.

"I'll do my best to move things along." Zach opened the door to the house and walked into the kitchen. Maybe Crystal did know how to paint if she was prepping the room.

He carried drop cloths up the steps and paused in the doorway. Crystal stood on the ladder, her heart-shaped ass facing him at about eye level. He swallowed hard, blood rushing south.

No.

Just no.

He'd been there one second, and his reactions to her were already causing trouble.

At least she'd worn a long sleeve shirt and pants. Functional clothing for the job. He had shorts and a T-shirt on, but he could afford to scrub his skin if paint dried on him. She didn't have that luxury with the rash.

Maybe her attire would help keep his overactive libido in check around her. Only he'd stared at her ass anyway.

When he tossed the drop cloths on the floor, she turned and smiled. "Oh, good, you're here. I'm almost done." She waved a hand around the room. "I think I got it all. I taped the edges of the carpet too, just in case."

That smile, a real one, not the for-the-camera kind, drew him in. The way it lit up her face, along with the pride in her voice, made *him* grin. And he didn't grin much. Never mind the "good, you're here" comment. When had she ever been happy to see him?

Her eyebrows raised, and her cheeks flushed.

"What?" he asked.

She shrugged. "You should do that more often."

"Do what?"

"Smile. Like I told you back at Urgent Care, you rarely do. Did you know studies have shown smiling makes you feel happier? There's an emotional connection with facial expressions. Scowling can have the opposite effect and make a person grumpier." She climbed down the ladder and stood in front of him.

"I don't know if I buy that."

"Don't believe me? Try it for yourself and see."

No way he'd walk around like a clown with a goofy grin on his face all day. Not happening.

She cocked her head. "What are you thinking right now?"

"Why do you want to know?"

"Because you look cranky again. I'm just trying to help, not force you to do anything you don't want. I like seeing people happy, but you don't seem like you are very often."

Guilt tightened a noose around his lungs. He never meant to bring anyone down with his moods. All the more reason to keep his distance from people and not burden them with pity. "You wouldn't understand."

"Maybe I would. Try me." She took a step closer, and her sweet scent filled his nostrils.

He couldn't afford to open himself up to her. That didn't fit with having boundaries. "Not now. We have a lot of work to do."

Crystal pointed to some cans of paint on the floor. "I think everything we need is there."

He squatted to check them out. Sure enough, all the right stuff. Go figure. "Looks good."

She had moved the bed and bureau away from the wall to tape the carpet. Again, thinking ahead. After taking a picture down, he pulled out the nail behind. "I'll have to spackle this hole, but we can get started."

Zach held the frame in his hands for a moment as memories flooded him.

"I take it that was someone special?" Crystal asked.

"Yes. My father." Zach ran a hand down the front of the picture. "This is him in his army uniform. He was my inspiration. Pretty much my hero growing up."

"Because of medals he earned?"

"Nope. Like most people in the military, he lived his life dedicated to the service and our family. A simple man with values and lessons to teach. It says a lot that he made lifelong friends in the army." The corners of Zach's mouth turned up. "I used to smear mud on my face and shoot my brothers with squirt guns to try to be like him."

"That's funny," Crystal said. "You told me you all pranked each other, but you must have gotten along."

He shrugged. "As much as three brothers could. Brody didn't

engage too much. He was always the serious one, afraid we'd get into trouble and damage something."

"Why?" Crystal's nose crinkled.

Damn if it wasn't the cutest thing he'd seen in a long while. The tiny freckles all cinched up. He found himself staring at them until Crystal broke his focus.

"Why did Brody worry?"

Zach tore his gaze from her face, back to the photo of his father. "Dad made us pay for stuff."

"What stuff?"

"Broken windows, knocked down fences, exterminator fees—"

"Oh my God. What on earth did you guys do?" She scanned the room as if searching for bugs.

"Everything. We were kids. You know, hit a baseball through a window, plant spiders in a bedroom...real ones, not rubber like yours for the tutors."

Her eyes grew wide, and he laughed again.

"It wasn't a big deal," he said. "We just worked extra chores as punishment. It was worth it because Levi and I pulled some epic pranks."

He followed her gaze around the room and put a reassuring hand on her arm. "That was a long time ago. No spiders here now."

Heat radiated to his fingers even through her shirt, and he drew his hand back. One touch, and she set him aflame.

Crystal peered again at the picture. "He sounds like an amazing father. You resemble him."

"I do?"

"For sure. You have his eyes."

Zach studied the picture. Maybe. He'd never noticed before. A warm vibe traveled up his body. "All I know is he was the glue of our family. Everyone looked up to him. You know how that goes. We all stick together."

Crystal touched the frame. "I think it's wonderful."

Shit.

What the heck had gotten into him? Crystal had told him about her good-for-nothing mother and non-existent father. She'd asked about the photo, but he shouldn't have rambled on about family, knowing she'd never had one. His face grew hot, and he blew out a breath.

"Hey, I'm sorry. I forgot—"

"Nothing to apologize for. I asked, and I appreciate you sharing. It makes me feel good to know you all support each other, especially your mom." She gave him a warm smile and picked up a drop cloth. "I suppose we should get to work?"

"Yes. We need to get this done as soon as possible." All this reminiscing was foreign to him. He needed to bring things back to neutral ground.

"I think we're set to go. By the way, good choice in clothing." He waved a hand at her pants.

Crystal stiffened and cringed.

She pulled her ballcap lower. "Yeah, I figured it would help."

Help? What did she mean by that?

Chapter Nineteen

C rystal bent over, hiding her face, to lay out the drop cloth. Shame warmed her skin, causing it to itch. Of course, he'd appreciate that she'd covered herself up. She'd forgotten about how she looked when he'd been talking about his family, opening up for the first time.

That made it all the worse because for a while there, he'd treated her like a normal person, not the celebrity who had an image to regain. She'd felt a connection to him beyond whatever chemistry they had going on when he'd shared his past. All the special memories and thoughts about his family. His eyes had softened when he'd spoken of his father, and Zach had even laughed and smiled at her more than once. She'd started to believe maybe, just maybe, he might have found her trustworthy, capable of seeing and feeling things deeper than surface value.

Only she should have known better. No one saw any worth beyond her appearance. Present company included. The painful reminder sliced her heart.

"I don't understand your comment about your clothes helping." Zach moved a can of paint out of the way. "Helping what?"

"Forget it. Let's just get this done because it's already warm in here." And her long sleeves and pants added to the discomfort.

Zach opened his mouth as if to say more, then shut it. He glanced around the room. "The primer will dry faster if we open the windows and use a fan, but you're not supposed to get too hot, so I'll wait and do it when we're done. The sooner we finish, the better."

She nodded.

Zach shook the primer. "I'll do the trim if you want to do the rolling?"

He wore one of his usual olive T-shirts, and her gaze fixated on the way his biceps bulged with every shake of the can. Her hormones flared at the sight.

"Will that work?" he asked.

"Uh, what?"

"You using the roller."

"Oh, sure." Crystal bit her lower lip and eyed the painting stuff. The helpful man in the hardware store had gathered up everything he thought they'd need. Otherwise, she'd have been clueless.

On the way back in the car, she'd watched some YouTube videos on how to prep. That was as far as she'd gotten. Still, how hard could it be?

Zach opened the lid. He poured primer into a paint tray with a liner and gestured across the room. "The roller's right there."

After filling an empty coffee can with paint, he turned his back to her and reached up to brush it on near the ceiling. Made sense for him to do it since he wouldn't need the ladder. She snatched the metal roller frame and slid on a fuzzy cylinder.

Nothing to it. She had this. Her gaze darted to Zach, and she stalled again. Now his broad shoulders flexed as he moved the brush across the wall. A hot flame ignited in her core. He caught her staring when he dipped the brush for more paint.

"What's wrong?" he asked.

"Nothing. I was...thinking about where to start." More like not thinking at all since her brain went on vacation when he got her stirred up.

He pointed to the doorway. "If you start there, we won't get in each other's way."

"Okay." She carried the tray over, coated the roller, and ran it up the wall. Drops of paint splattered on her shirt. Oops. She slowed down and glanced at Zach. Phew. He hadn't noticed.

Two more swipes with no problems. She sighed in relief. Once she got into a rhythm, she finished three walls in short order. "This isn't so hard."

Zach turned around. "You sound surprised. When's the last time you did this?"

Uh oh. Busted. "I can't even remember." Not a total lie. She dipped the roller again to avoid his scrutiny and made another pass.

"What's this?" Zach asked. "I almost stepped on it, doing the ceiling trim."

She swung around as he picked up a sketchpad she'd left on the floor.

Damn.

While Erin was making dinner earlier, Crystal had played with colors and dabbed paint beside the flowers she'd drawn. They'd stopped at a craft store on the way back from town, and she'd picked up everything she'd need for stenciling. She'd meant to stash the sketchbook away but had forgotten. At some point, Zach would see the final product, but she never shared her works-in-progress with anyone and didn't know what he'd think.

"It's nothing. I'll get it out of your way." She reached for the pad. He held it tight, studying the page.

"These flower sketches are amazing. Did you draw this?"

"Well, yeah. Like I said, I do paint."

"I'm impressed. Did you take art lessons?" he asked.

A wave of pride soared through her. "No, I taught myself. I plan to come back and detail the walls after everything dries." She waved a hand around the room. "I'm going to sketch these flowers along the borders, and they'll blend with the pictures your mom and I picked out today at the thrift store. She seems so excited to have a pretty room to host her friends."

Zach rubbed the side of his face. "Okay, one thing at a time. First of all, *you* went to a thrift store?"

Crystal flinched. "Are you judging me? Your mother wanted to go there. We found some nice—"

"No. I'm not judging you. I'm just...surprised."

She peered up from under her cap. "Why?"

"Doesn't seem like the kind of store you'd shop in. And I'd think you'd have been worried about someone recognizing you."

He was right on both counts. She shrugged. "I wore a hat, sunglasses, and these clothes."

"Huh."

"Turns out, there are a lot of nice things in the shop if you have a discerning eye, and we found the perfect pictures for this room without costing your mother a fortune." She nodded in satisfaction.

He let out a breath. "Well, good. Moving on to the next subject. Exactly how do you plan to detail this room when the paint isn't going to be dry until Friday, and company is coming on Saturday?"

Crystal nibbled her lip. "I have it all worked out, no need to worry."

His gaze dropped to her mouth, and a muscle under his jaw twitched.

"I better stop talking or we'll never finish. I'll—"

"Not so fast." He shook his head. "Enlighten me on this plan of yours."

Crap. He wouldn't let this go, but it didn't matter. She was bound and determined to finish the room. "Levi said he'd lend me his bike. It has a headlight, and this is just a couple miles off the island. Sydney can't possibly bitch if I leave when it's dark because they aren't filming then." Crystal straightened her shoulders. "I can get the job done in less than two hours and have it ready for Saturday morning, no problem."

Zach held his breath and counted to five. "To be clear, your plan is to ride a bike, with just a headlight, down dark country roads for miles?"

"There shouldn't be much traffic. Deer would be the only issue, and I won't be going fast like a car."

"Not that this is *ever* happening, but which side of the road would you be riding on?"

"The right side, of course. Do you think I'm an idiot?"

"No. You'd be surprised at how many bikers don't know they are supposed to be on the same side as the cars driving." He grazed a hand down his face. "Oncoming traffic in the opposite lane will see the headlight, but you need a taillight for the cars behind you."

She frowned. "I'm really not worried about it. In the dark, anyone should be able to see a headlight."

"Never mind. You're making me crazy. There's no way you're riding a bike here at night. It's not safe. I can't bring you because I'll have a camp full of Boy Scouts."

The tension in her chest eased. Great. Problem solved. She didn't want to spend more time with him anyway. All he did was make her feel things she'd rather not, considering their attraction was going nowhere.

Zach frowned. "You can borrow my truck."

"Thanks, but no way. I haven't driven much in my life and wouldn't be comfortable handling something that big. Your mom wanted to pick me up, but she said she's not supposed to drive in the dark with her bad night vision. Don't worry about it. I'll be fine." Crystal turned, but he put a hand on her arm.

"Wait a second. Are you saying my mother is okay with this? You told her what you're going to do?" The side of his mouth twisted.

"Yup. Now, we should get back to—"

"Hold on." Zach went to the top of the stairs. "Hey, Mom?"

Chapter Twenty

Z ach waited, glancing at Crystal from the corner of his eye. No way his mother was okay with Crystal riding a bike on pitch-dark roads at night.

"What?" His mom came to the bottom of the steps.

"Did Crystal tell you how she was going to get here Friday night to paint flowers on the walls?"

"Yes, it's very sweet of her." His mother wiped her hands on the dishtowel she held. "Oh, and Crystal, I'd like to go with the fuchsia pink you showed me. Do you think that will work?"

"Of course. That's my favorite."

The acid in his stomach burned. Had an alien taken over his mother? She thought Crystal's plan was "sweet," not dangerous?

His mom called up the stairs, "And by the way, Crystal, no need for you to ride a bike here. I couldn't live with myself if anything happened to you. Brody is coming on Friday night to discuss the finances for the farm stand and co-op sales. He said he'd bring you and take you back."

Crystal's face fell before she pasted on a polite smile. "That's nice of him. Thanks."

Zach's tight muscles eased. At least that problem was resolved. He stepped back into the bedroom.

Crystal followed, tugging her hat lower. Why did she keep doing that? It was not like the sun was shining in her eyes. Whatever. Time was ticking, and he needed to get busy.

He flashed back to the happy smile on his mom's face after shopping with Crystal. "I don't decorate, so thanks for doing all this for my mother."

"Well, I...I'm doing it for you too. You're nice enough to let me stay at your place." Crystal toyed with a button on her shirt.

The tentative way she'd said it and the redness in her cheeks tugged at his heart.

"We're both grateful. It's warm in here even with the air on. Why don't you roll up your sleeves and pants?"

"It's all right. I don't want to..."

"You don't want to what?" He took a step closer.

She kept her head down.

"Crystal? What are you trying not to say?"

"I'm glad you agreed to let me help. The least I can do is try not to gross you out."

"What are you talking about?"

"The way I look. You said it yourself. You appreciate me wearing these clothes. And your mom's comment about how hard it was for you to be around me." Her voice caught. "I'm not blind. I'm ugly right now."

"Wait a minute." He scratched his head. Was she out of her mind? It was taking a monumental effort for him not to stare at her. "I said that about your outfit because I thought you were being smart, covering up so you wouldn't get paint on your skin."

She looked him in the eyes for a quick second. "What about what your mom said? And why did you race out of your house earlier when she was making those comments?"

Zach shook his head. He had no idea what got into Crystal. She was saying things that made no sense, and he couldn't take anymore. "It's true I find it hard to be around you, but not for the reason you think."

"It's not because I disgust you?"

He blinked. "That's what you think?"

She dipped her head again. "Well...yeah. I mean, I can't blame you."

"Stop doing that." He put a finger under her chin and raised her head. "You don't have to hide your face from me."

She blushed. "It's a mess. Bright pink."

"It would take a hell of a lot more than that to make you unattractive." His gaze followed the sweet curve of her neck. He stroked his thumb under her chin. "You are beautiful to me, splotchy face or not."

She trembled. Her lips parted, and she moistened them. The tiny flick of her tongue sent a coil of heat to his belly, and his cock came to life. Her eyes darkened as the air between them sizzled. "You're just being nice."

He slid the hat off her head and threaded his fingers through the back of her hair. "Don't believe me? Let me prove it."

Inch by inch, he lowered his head, pulling her against his body.

Her nipples hardened when they pressed on his chest, and he captured her mouth in a kiss.

Soft and slow, he moved his mouth over hers.

She wrapped her arms around his neck and kissed him back.

Heat blazed inside, fueling his desire. He slid his tongue along her teeth, and she opened for him.

She tasted of sweet mint, and he couldn't get enough of her. He thrust his tongue deeper, exploring every corner of her mouth. A small whimper escaped her, and his ever-growing hard-on strained against the fabric of his pants.

His heart pumped faster than a high-speed train and took him right off the rails. He cupped her ass with his hands, and she moaned, digging her nails into his back.

She rocked her hips, and he groaned.

Someone cleared their throat from the doorway.

Zach froze, and Crystal jerked away from him.

Her eyes were wide, and her lips swollen. She gasped for air and stumbled backward, right into Levi.

"I came to see if Crystal wanted a ride home, but it looks like she's in good hands." Levi gave Zach a sideways grin and steadied her, letting go when she found her balance.

Zach's entire body was on fire. What the holy hell? He clearly couldn't trust himself to be around her. He bent and picked up the paintbrush to avoid facing her. "It's hot, and I'm almost done. Just go ahead, Crystal."

She mumbled something and bolted past Levi.

Zach pointed to him. "Not a word from you."

Levi shook his head, a rueful, you-just-blew-it smile on his face before he turned and followed Crystal.

Zach's shoulders slumped. How the hell was he going to fix this?

Chapter Twenty-One

Crystal's heart raced as she stood by the car, waiting for Levi. What was wrong with her? She'd lost control. At the touch of Zach's lips, her body had cranked into full lust mode, craving him. She'd never been kissed that way before. She couldn't get close enough, and she'd sure as hell tried.

At least it hadn't been one-sided.

The kicker was he'd kissed her even though she looked like she'd fallen face-first into a hornet's nest. She wore no makeup, had blotchy skin, and hat hair. No guy in Hollywood would have come close to her, much less have kissed her.

Zach had told her he didn't care about her splotchy face. She wouldn't have believed him if he hadn't backed it up with a kiss.

And what a kiss.

Levi came out of the house, and they climbed into the car. He started the engine. "You sure you want to leave?"

"Yes. Please, can we get out here?" She buried her face in her hands.

"All right." He backed the car out of the driveway. "You wanna talk about it?"

"I'm mortified," she said, her voice muffled through her fingers. She'd humiliated herself enough for one night.

A strangled chuckle came from the driver's seat, and she whipped her head up. "What's so funny?"

"I'm sorry. I can't help it. Zach and Brody have given me endless shit over my love life, and it's nice to have the tables turned for once. I don't mean to be a jerk. I can see you're embarrassed, but you and Zach are adults. It's not like you got caught kissing on the playground." He nudged her arm. "It's okay to admit you like each other."

"But we don't. We drive each other crazy. He orders me around all the time and treats me like a child. And all I do is cause trouble."

"Uh huh." Levi slowed for a stop sign and glanced at her. "Trust me, he does *not* think of you as a child."

The memory of Zach's tongue sliding against hers and his hands cupping her ass sent a wave of heat through her. She angled her body and gazed out the window to hide what had to be a full-out blush.

"And the ordering you around thing? Zach was a combat engineer in charge of a unit overseas. He's used to telling people what to do, including Brody and me, but we don't put up with it."

"I didn't know what he did in the army."

"Even I don't know much about it. All I can say is he had a tough time over there and came back different."

"Does he have PTSD?" Maybe that would explain some of his behaviors. The need for control and following all the safety rules.

"He wouldn't want me talking about it. Maybe just cut him some slack if he's testy at times."

Crystal's heart hurt as she pictured the photos of Zach growing up with huge grins. He sure didn't smile much now.

Levi drove past the gate. "I'm taking you to Zach's, right?"

"Yeah, but the sooner I leave there, the better. I don't know what to do. I'm supposed to help him paint tomorrow night. I won't let your mother down." But Crystal couldn't imagine spending more one-on-one time with him after the night's catastrophe.

Levi pulled into Zach's driveway. "Don't you think you two should try to kiss and make up?"

She shook her head fast and hard. "No. I'm not going to be here much longer. There's no point. Tonight was a big mistake, and now it's an awkward mess, but I'll figure it out. I appreciate the ride and didn't mean to dump on you."

"You're not dumping." Levi waved a hand. "Truth is, I was jerking Zach's chain with that offer of a ride. I thought a little competition might help."

"How?"

"I told you he has a thing for you. I figured he'd get jealous." Levi shrugged.

"That backfired. He leaped at the chance to get rid of me. He doesn't want me around," Crystal said.

"I think you're wrong about that."

"Even if I am, after what you just told me, all I can do is hurt him. I have nothing long-term to offer." She brushed a hand down her pants and willed her breath not to catch. "Unless I'm wrong, neither of us is looking for a fling, and the closer we get, the harder it will be on both of us when I leave. Am I right?"

Levi closed his eyes and nodded. "Yeah, I guess you are."

"That's what I figured." They sat in silence for a second. Crystal opened the car door. "Thanks again for the ride."

"Wait." Levi tugged her sleeve. "I'm not doing anything tomorrow night. I can help Zach paint."

Crystal's chest expanded with relief. "You'd do that for me?"

Levi nodded. "For both of you, and Mom."

"Thanks so much." Crystal gave his fingers a quick squeeze. "I promise I'll go back on Friday night to do the detailing. You're a good friend and brother."

"Let's keep that our secret. I have a reputation to maintain." Levi winked at her.

"Night, Levi." Crystal stepped out of the car and headed to the house.

"Holy shit," Levi shouted. "I can't believe it."

"What?" Crystal whirled around and took a few steps back.

Levi laughed long and hard. He leaned his head against the steering wheel and held his belly, coming up for air long enough to point to the window AC unit. "He bought a freaking air conditioner."

"I know. I'm going to pay him—"

"Good luck with that. You have no idea what a big deal this is." Levi's eyes lit up and a big grin split his face. "Oh, he's got it bad for you. This is far from over."

Chapter Twenty-Two

Zach finished his rounds and stopped the UTV by a quiet part of the lake not far from Crystal's camp. He'd managed to avoid her for two days. Not hard to do when she was cooped up in his house. She'd texted him earlier that she was well enough to come back to work, so he'd cleared out of her space.

What was he going to do about her? His chest muscles tightened and pinched his ribs. History showed he had zero control around her. He'd kissed her senseless and grabbed her ass in his *mother's* house.

What the hell?

If Levi hadn't interrupted them, who knew how far things might have gone? Crystal's response to the kiss had shocked Zach. He'd gone from zero to sixty the second she'd opened her mouth and leaned into him.

He raked a hand over his head. Crystal drove him up a freaking wall. When she'd said he must think she was ugly, he'd been speechless. He'd never found her more attractive. She didn't grasp that what he saw in her had nothing to do with flawless skin and a painted-on face. She'd followed through with her promise to detail the room, coming back Friday night, when she had to have been exhausted. His mom had sent pictures of the flower border and was thrilled.

The more he got to know Crystal, the deeper he sank. Like it or not, she was working her way into his heart.

Meanwhile, Levi had piled on the guilt when he'd come to help finish the paint job. He'd told Zach how upset Crystal was and accused him of acting like an adolescent. He didn't need lectures from his playboy brother.

Maybe Levi had a point, as much as it killed him to admit it. Ghosting Crystal wasn't the most mature way to handle a problem. He needed to thank her for making the room beautiful, clear the air, and keep his damned hands off her.

Movement by the lake caught his eye. Crystal stood on the shore with a fishing rod. No camera crew around and she was outside of camp. She wore khaki pants and a long-sleeved floral shirt. Maybe the sensible clothing would help keep his overactive libido in check. But, that hadn't worked when they'd painted together.

He hiked closer and paused as she cast a line and reeled it in fast. She must be using a lure, although he'd found that the best bait for bream in shallow water was night crawlers.

Didn't matter. Right now, he needed to talk to her. He stepped through the brush, making sure she could hear him approach so he wouldn't startle her.

She turned, caught her breath, and pursed her lips, facing the lake again. "What do you want?"

"To talk to you." He stopped a few feet away and crossed his arms. She snorted. "Nice body language. Doesn't look like it."

Shit.

He uncrossed his arms and checked out the exposed parts of her skin. Relief washed through him. The meds must have worked because the rash was almost gone. "I'm here to thank you for helping my mother and to clear the air."

Her shoulders stiffened, and she faced him. "You're welcome, and what do you mean clear the air?"

"This thing we have for each other isn't going anywhere because you're leaving soon. I don't want to make you uncomfortable during the time that's left. Can we please put what happened behind us?"

She lowered her head, studying the grass, or mud, or maybe her feet. After a second, she nodded. "You're right. We should."

"Okay, then?" he asked, unsure of how easily she'd accepted his words. So unlike her not to argue.

"Yup, all good." She grabbed her fishing rod and squinted at the worm wriggling on the hook.

Way too big. That's what she'd been casting and reeling in fast? His brain screamed at him. *Walk away.* But he couldn't. "What are you doing?"

"I'm practicing fishing because we're filming this scene later. Why?"

"You're not going to catch one like this. You have to—"

"I admit I don't know what I'm doing, but I watched some YouTube videos, and I have to try. You aren't allowed to help me, Zach." She lowered the worm into the water. "Poor thing. I hate this."

His heart wrenched for her. He knew what it was like to have to do something that went against his nature. Came with the territory, being in the army. "Hold tight. I'll be back in a bit."

"What for?"

He waved a hand and headed to the UTV. He might not be able to help her, but he could show by example. Maybe he needed his head examined because he'd sworn he was going to clear the air and stay away from her. Yet, he couldn't. He appreciated her grit and determination. Something he hadn't expected from her. She deserved a fair chance, and he'd give her one.

Back at his house, he grabbed his fishing gear, bait, and a cooler of ice.

He parked a distance away from the area since he didn't know when Sydney and Trevor were supposed to show up. When he reached Crystal, he noted that she'd switched to an artificial lure, which was still way too big.

She shook her head. "What are you doing? I don't understand. You aren't allowed to help me, and I don't want to break any rules and hurt your business."

That made him want to help her all the more. "I'm gonna fish."

"Right here?" She gestured to where he stood. "There's an entire lake and you're going to fish right freaking *here*?"

"Yup. No law against it." He opened a container of worms and pulled one out. "Huh. This is too big." He broke the worm in half, and Crystal gasped.

"Oh my God. That's mean. Why did you do that?"

He cocked his head. "You ever order a burger that came out bigger than you could open your mouth to take a bite?"

"No, but I've seen those before in restaurants."

"Think about it. What size fish are you trying to catch?"

She blinked a couple of times, then grinned. "Got it."

His belly flopped. So much for not reacting to her.

He made a point of holding up the hook as he threaded it through the worm so she could see what to do.

She winced. "A colonoscopy?"

"Never thought of it that way." He laughed and plucked a bobber from his tackle box. After attaching it, he cinched on a weight and cast the line.

Crystal checked out her tackle box. She slipped on a pair of latex gloves.

He bit the side of his tongue to keep from making wisecracks.

She mimicked what he'd done with his line. Her face contorted like she was witnessing an autopsy as she baited the hook. "Sorry, sorry, sorry."

A pang of sympathy went through Zach at the way Crystal cared about hurting the worm.

She cast. In less than a minute, her bobber twitched.

"A fish!" She reeled fast, but the line went slack. "Dang it."

"Patience," he said.

Crystal pointed to his bobber, which jiggled. "Something's biting yours."

Zach waited. Two more twitches. He reeled in the slack. When the bobber plunged underwater, he jerked his pole in the opposite direction to set the hook. The rod bent, and he reeled in a fish. A pumpkinseed sunfish about the size of his hand.

He unhooked and tossed it into the cooler.

"I saw pictures of those online. Their bright orange color is so pretty." She brushed her hair back with her forearm and sighed. "I get it. I was too quick before. Now that I see how to do it, I know I can."

He rebaited his hook and recast. "Of course you can."

"Another fish." She froze when her bobber bounced again.

This time she waited, and sure enough, it went under. She yanked her rod like he'd done and brought in the fish.

"Oh my God, I did it." She jumped up and down.

The fish swung from the end of the rod.

Another pumpkinseed, about the same size as Zach's. He couldn't help but smile at her exuberance. "That's a nice one."

"It is. But now I have to clean it."

Zach steeled himself. If she was grossed out by threading a worm, she'd die a slow death gutting a fish. "I'll do mine too."

"You will?" Her eyebrows shot up.

Her pink face, flushed from excitement, made something of *his* twitch. He had to shut that right down. Shoving a hand into the ice, he pulled out his fish.

Crystal had managed to unhook hers and held it tightly in her gloved hand.

He picked up a filet knife and placed the fish on top of the cooler. Crystal grabbed her knife and pointed to a flat-topped tree stump. He nodded. That would work.

He cut off the head, and she wrinkled her nose, eyes wide.

Her fish wiggled as she pressed it down with her hand. She whimpered, then sliced the head off and squeezed her eyes shut. "I can't look at it."

"Breathe, Crystal."

She took a shaky breath and opened her lids. "Okay."

The fish had stopped moving, and she peeked at Zach.

This next part wasn't going to sit well with her. He sliced the fish open, reached inside, and pulled out the entrails.

"Eww, eww, eww." Her face turned ghost-white, and she shook her head hard. "I read about how to do this, but I didn't want to see the videos. It's grosser than I even thought."

Still, he had to give it to her, she was hanging in there. "It's a small fish. You can do it."

She whimpered more, but cut the stomach open, gagging as she reached inside. She took out the innards and flung them to the ground. "Gross." Her face squinched in disgust. She stomped her feet, shook her hands, and yelled at the fish, "I hate your guts."

Zach burst out laughing. He couldn't help it. She was dancing around like she was on fire.

Crystal shuddered and pouted, her eyes watering. "It's not funny. I feel sorry for the poor little thing."

His gaze went to her trembling lip, and a spring of heat unfurled in his belly. He fought the urge to kiss her senseless. He cursed to himself. How could he be turned on by her while cleaning a damn fish? And she was upset, which made him a horrible person. A horrible, horny person. He wiped the grin off his face and softened his voice. "The first time you do this is the hardest. Trust me, that fish died fast. You're doing great."

She sniffled and gave him a watery smile. "Thanks."

"Almost done." He grabbed a butter knife, held the tail down, and scraped the scales forward.

Following suit, she did the same. "This part isn't so bad."

"Nothing left to do but fry it. Do you know how?"

"Yeah. I watched some videos. I think I'll impress Sydney and Trevor. They won't know I practiced." She turned to him, her blue eyes shining. "Thanks for this. You've saved me from mega humiliation later."

His shoulders tensed. She still didn't understand. He had to try again to tell her about the producer's plans.

Crystal's phone beeped, and she picked it up.

"Shit. They're on the way. You gotta get out of here." She ripped off her gloves, grabbed her fish, and shoved both at him. "Take these. They can't know I caught this or see the bloody carnage."

"All right, but there's something I need to—"

"Go, now." She tossed the knives in the tackle box and slammed the lid shut.

Zach chucked the fish into the cooler and picked up his gear. Frantic, she snagged her equipment and hurried to another spot farther along the shore.

With a ragged sigh, he headed in the opposite direction. When would he see her alone again to be able to talk?

Chapter Twenty-Three

C rystal yawned and rolled over in her sleeping bag. Her hair stuck to her face and pillow from the humidity. She missed Zach's bed. The way his scent clung to the sheets and lingered in the house. She'd never slept better.

As always, she woke up thinking about him. She hadn't known what to say when he'd said he wanted to clear the air. Some part of her had hoped...what? His logic made sense. No point in getting involved when she was leaving soon. He seemed to have no problem "putting it all behind them."

If only she could.

But he'd been clear, and she wouldn't grovel and tell him that what she felt went beyond attraction.

He'd taken precious time out of his day to teach her to fish, saving her from humiliation. And he'd been kind and patient the whole time. Even after he'd laughed at her, he'd backed off and made her feel proud. Her chest tingled with longing. They'd had fun together during the grossest experience of her life.

Thanks to him, Crystal rocked the fishing scene. She caught two sunfish, cleaned, and cooked them. Even with her acting skills, she couldn't control her facial expressions at the revulsion of the task, but she hadn't lost her shit like the first time. No hopping, flailing, or yelling at creatures.

Sydney was satisfied they'd had two days of successful shoots. Crystal had fished, hiked, and started a campfire. She'd struggled to light the flame, but it wasn't too embarrassing, so she'd approve the scene.

Crystal needed a breath of air to get her mind off Zach. She stepped out of the tent and glanced at the camp next door. Johnny faced his sister, holding Murphy's leash as the dog sniffed the ground.

"Mom said I could walk him alone this morning as long as I didn't go too far." His voice rang with pride.

Angie rubbed her eyes and snarled, "Better watch out. A black bear's been spotted. You'd be a tasty appetizer, small as you are."

Crystal broke out in a sweat. A bear in the area? Zach had warned her about them.

The boy petted the dog. "I'm not scared. Me and Murphy can handle anything."

"Murphy's no match for a grizzly. The bear will take him out with one swipe of its claws." Angie curled her hand and made a slashing motion.

Johnny wrapped an arm around the dog and hugged him. "No way."

"Just saying." Angie smirked. "If mom asks, I checked on you as ordered. Now, I'm going back to bed."

Crystal's blood pressure spiked. Why was that girl so mean to her little brother? She snagged one of the whistles she'd bought and marched outside.

"Hey," she called to Johnny.

Murphy lunged at the sound of her voice and dragged the child to her. The dog ran in circles around her feet, tail wagging hard.

Johnny tried to rein in the dog. "Sorry ma'am. He gets excited around people."

She glanced at Murphy, who had a sloppy tongue hanging from

the side of his mouth. Big dogs really needed to be trained, but at least he was friendly.

Crystal smiled at Johnny. Ma'am? Guess she would look old to a child. She held out the whistle. "I read if you blow this while you're in the woods, it will scare off bears."

"Really? Thanks." He took it and blew hard several times. Murphy cocked his head.

"You like the sound?" Johnny tooted it three more times and laughed.

His sister yelled from inside the tent, "Stop blowing that thing. I'm trying to sleep."

Crystal bent down and whispered. "Maybe it will work on grumpy people too."

"She hates camping. All her friends go to the beach for vacation." He ruffled the fur on Murphy's head. "I think it's fun here."

"Well, enjoy yourself and don't let her ruin it." Crystal straightened and went back into her tent. That girl should appreciate her caring family, regardless of where they went. But she'd have nothing to compare it to, being raised by loving parents. If she only knew what it was like to be left with some paid-by-the-hour caretaker, who didn't give a crap about her. Crystal didn't wish that on anyone and couldn't blame Angie for what she didn't know. But still, the girl should be nicer to her brother.

Crystal opened two boxes Sydney had dropped off. She grinned at the glamping decor inside. A string of triangle flags with bright-colored floral patterns, a turquoise feathered dreamcatcher, and some solar-powered lights. Her belly danced as she stepped outside and draped the lights on her tent. She tied the flag banner to the branches of a few trees. Perfect. She took a picture and created a new post.

Trevor was meeting her by the lake to film a kayaking scene, so she hung the dreamcatcher inside the tent and then changed clothes.

She slung a whistle over her head. Best to be safe.

As she trudged through the woods, she blew it every few steps.

She spied Trevor and Sydney standing near the lake ahead. Their heads turned in her direction when she blew the whistle a couple more times.

A loud rustling noise came from behind.

"Bear! Bear!" a man's gruff voice bellowed.

Crystal whipped around, spotting something big and black headed straight for her. Her lungs slammed against her ribs as terror gripped her.

Oh my God! Oh my God! Oh my God!

The bear was after her.

Adrenaline spiked through her body as she scanned the woods. Her gaze locked on a tall tree ahead with low branches.

Her heart raced even faster than the first time she'd walked the red carpet. She threw everything to the ground and sprinted to the tree, a surge of energy boosting her speed.

She grabbed a branch and pulled her body up, feet scrambling for a hold.

Limb after limb, she climbed higher and higher until she ran out of sturdy boughs.

Wrapping her arms around the trunk, her butt resting on a branch, she collapsed against the bark, gasping for air.

Could that bear climb up after her? Her insides quaked as she fumbled for her whistle.

She had to scare him off.

With a shaky hand, she brought it to her mouth and blew with all the air she had left.

Over and over, until she ran out of breath.

Sweat poured down her chest, and her vision blurred.

"Hey lady, you okay?" a man yelled from below.

She peered down.

Wayyyy down.

Chills tracked up her spine, and she gripped the tree tighter. The bark cut into her slick hands. Guess she had a fear of heights. Nice time to find out.

She blinked. Sweat dripped into her eyes, blurring her vision. With a death grip on the tree, she chanced another glance down.

A heavy-set guy stood below, holding the leash of a humungous black...dog?

The animal was bigger than a Saint Bernard and had a huge head and shaggy, long hair.

"I'm sorry if Bear scared you. Are you all right?" the man called.

So there had been a bear. She tried to concentrate, confusion muddling her mind. Why was he standing there if the bear was on the loose? "No. Where is the bear?"

"He's right here."

She took a deep breath and shook her head to clear it. "What? You yelled a warning about a bear."

"I was calling him because he got loose. He's big, but he'd never hurt anyone."

Someone giggled, and she glanced in the direction of the sound. Sydney stood beside Trevor, who had his camera pointed up the tree.

Crystal's nerves shattered, sending tiny shocks to her fingers. She dug them deeper into the bark.

The man turned his head, seeming to notice Trevor and Sydney for the first time. "Why are y'all filming this? Am I in trouble for having a loose dog? Bear doesn't usually get out."

Crystal squeezed her eyes shut, trying to process everything before gazing back at the guy.

"Wait, are you saying this dog is named Bear?"

"Yeah, 'cause he looks like one." The man nodded and grinned.

No shit.

Her legs and arms shook as she tried to keep a firm hold on the tree.

No bear. Just a dog named Bear. Relief was short-lived as she gauged her distance from the ground. She'd never be able to climb down. The only way she'd made it up was the fight-or-flight response that kicked into high gear, and now she was exhausted.

Lights flashed, and a police car rolled up to the nearby road. Followed by another.

Thank God. Help was on the way. Someone must have called 911. She rested her head against the tree and fought off a dizzy spell.

She couldn't look down anymore. It freaked her out.

When the cops arrived, they asked some questions about her condition, and she answered to the best of her ability. Their voices floated up to her like she was in some space bubble. If only.

Her arms prickled, and she slanted an eye open.

She gasped at the sight of ants crawling all over them.

Chapter Twenty-Four

Z ach drove the perimeter of his camp and tried to banish thoughts of Crystal from his brain. He'd watched them film her fishing scene from across the lake and had been proud of her. She'd used his method to catch fish, and damn if she hadn't looked confident and sure of herself. He'd cheered inside when she'd reeled in a couple. She'd caught, cleaned, and cooked them without wearing gloves. As squeamish as she was, that took guts.

He hadn't been able to see her face from the distance, but he'd bet she'd squinched it up in that cute, disgusted way. To her credit, she hadn't stomped her feet or flung her hands.

Two days had passed since then, and the producers had kept her busy, making up for lost time no doubt. More promotional gifts must have come in for Crystal because her tent glowed with solar lights, and she'd hung a flag banner. It gave the place a homey and fun vibe. Even though Crystal hated camping, she was trying to make the best of things.

He stopped the UTV in a shady spot and took a sip of water. A yearning tugged at his heart. He'd wanted to see her face when she'd brought in those fish. And when she'd gutted and scaled them. And when she'd fried them up and took her first bite. And when she'd opened the glamping decorations, he could picture her eyes dancing with excitement. This wasn't going anywhere good. He had to stop thinking about her. Obsessing was more accurate.

Setting the canteen back in the cup holder, he pressed the accelerator. When he rounded the corner to Crystal's camp, he spotted two police cars with lights flashing.

His stomach flipped and crash landed. Had something happened to her?

He jumped from the UTV and surveyed the scene. Several people stood at the bottom of a tall maple tree, looking up. Trevor, Sydney, a man with a huge black dog, and three cops. Zach spotted Crystal high in the tree, arms wrapped around the trunk.

An electric shock ripped through his chest. A million questions barraged his brain, but he shoved them aside. First things first. He hurried to the cops. "I run this camp. What's going on here?"

A police officer turned and told him they had called dispatch for a ladder truck and EMTs since the woman sounded pretty shaky.

"How long until they get here?" Zach asked.

"We just radioed it in. Haven't heard back yet," the cop said.

Zach squinted up at Crystal. She was flailing a hand, swiping at her arm. Shit. She was panicking. If she didn't keep her focus, she might fall, and that was a hell of a long way down.

He ticked through his options at warp speed and did what he always did in a crisis.

Took action.

No time for standing around when she was in danger. If nothing else, he'd secure her until the truck arrived.

He grasped a branch and hoisted himself up. He'd climbed more trees than he could count growing up, and his military training included rescue missions carrying people, so he had this.

Sydney yelled from below.

He ignored her and focused on Crystal.

Limb after limb, he scaled the tree. "Hold on and breathe. I'm coming for you."

"Wh-what? Zach?"

Her shrill, thin voice told him all he needed to know, and he climbed faster, sure-footed on the branches. "Hang on."

At last, he reached the limb below her. Her pale, sweaty face spoke for itself. Her breath was shallow, and her legs shook.

"You're going to be okay. Look at me."

She gulped air and glanced down at him. Her wide eyes lasered in on his.

"Good. That's good." Sweat slicked his back. Her foggy gaze meant she was in trouble.

"The fire ants. The phenamores. They're attacking me." She frantically swiped at her arm.

She meant pheromones, but that wasn't the point right now. "Stop flailing and calm down."

"I can't. They're everywhere." She brushed her arm, lost her grip on the tree trunk, and slipped off the branch.

As if in slow-motion, the next second stretched out, defying real time. Her mouth gaped as she let out a shriek, arms windmilling as she tried to grab onto anything solid.

Following pure instinct, he locked his arm over the limb above and caught her, pinning her body to him.

Damn, that had been too close. Adrenaline pumped through him, and he planted his legs, keeping a tight grip on her.

"I got you. You're okay. Don't move."

More lights flashed below as the fire truck pulled up, along with an ambulance.

Relief flooded him. He could carry her down if she wasn't so freaked. Best to stay put.

Her heart pounded against his chest, and she clung to him, shaking.

"Trust me, and try to relax," he whispered against her ear.

She shuddered and took a long breath.

"That's good. Now let that out slowly." He kept a tight grip on her.

The rescue team below called out instructions, and he answered back. He'd keep her safe until they brought up the ladder.

"I don't want the ants to get you." She wriggled.

He hugged her tighter. "Stay still. They aren't fire ants. We're both fine."

She wasn't making any sense. Only it made perfect sense. Sometimes people focused on the lesser of two evils to keep their minds off imminent danger.

"The firefighters are here with a ladder. They're coming to help you down." He eyed the woman standing at the top of the ladder as it raised.

Crystal bit her lip. "I can't get on that. I'm scared."

"No need to be. They're professionals. You got this."

"I do?"

"Damn straight. You're a rock star. You climbed this sucker. Getting down is the easy part." He nodded to the firefighter, who'd come closer.

Crystal swallowed. "Yes, I did. And I got up here fast."

"No doubt. That's a story I'd like to hear later."

She glanced at the ladder. "I'm terrified of letting go of you to get on there."

"You'll be okay. They know what they are doing."

She rested her head on his shoulder. "How come you're never scared of anything?"

"Who ever said that?"

"No one. Just saying I've never seen you frightened."

More like he never *let* anyone see that side. If she only knew how terrified he was of losing it.

She lifted her head. "Tell me one thing you're afraid of."

His vocal cords tightened. He never talked about this, but she seemed to need to hear that even he had insecurities. "Flashbacks. I've had some tough times since my tour. So yeah, I have fears too."

"Oh, I'm sorry. That must be hard." Her lower lip came out and she rubbed his back, still clinging to him. "Thanks for sharing. I was starting to think you were Superman."

If so, Zach's kryptonite was his memory.

The firefighter, near now, called out some instructions.

Crystal hesitated.

Zach squeezed her. "You got this."

"Okay. You're right."

As panicked as she was, she got a hold of herself and followed directions. Maybe hearing he had an Achille's heel had helped. When she was secured on the ladder, Zach heaved a sigh. His pulse still raced from the aftermath of the adrenaline rush.

Crystal gazed at him and gave a thumbs up.

He nodded.

She mouthed "Thank you," and his heart rocked.

The firefighter said something about coming back for him. He shook his head, knowing he'd be fine to climb down on his own.

And then it all hit him.

The flashing lights from all the emergency vehicles. The close call that could have meant Crystal's life. The once-safe haven of his camp had turned into the circus he'd tried so hard to avoid.

He forced himself to go mission cold as the all-too-familiar feelings welled up inside. No way he'd have an episode perched in the tree and surrounded by people. He climbed down, fast and hard.

Brody stood next to Sydney. He must have driven up at some point.

As soon as Zach's feet touched the ground, Sydney launched into him. "Why are you always interfering? Keep out of our show or it's going to cost you. We can't use a lot of this because of your superhero shit."

That word again. Great. And in front of Brody, no less.

Sydney stomped toward the ambulance where Crystal was being checked out.

Zach braced himself, prepared for the inevitable onslaught from his big brother.

Brody shifted and cleared his throat. "You okay?"

"What?" Zach fought to keep his focus, but the chaos had every nerve on edge. He had to leave before a full-out episode ensued.

"Let's talk in private." Brody headed into the woods, and Zach followed.

When they reached the lake, he stopped and took a breath. Better.

Brody glanced back at the campsite, then faced Zach. "I'm sorry about this situation. I didn't realize what an impact having the show filmed here would have on you."

"It's all right. I just need a second." Zach held up a hand, his pulse slowing.

Brody waited a beat, slid his sunglasses up on his head, and looked Zach in the eyes. "You saved Crystal's life. I saw her fall. It's a damn good thing you *were* the superhero today."

"Not everyone sees it that way."

"Too bad." Brody grimaced. "Sydney can French kiss a cobra. I got your back."

Warmth spread through Zach, soothing his frayed nerves. His brother was standing up for him instead of arguing.

"You sure you're okay?" Brody asked.

"Yeah." The panic had subsided. Now he wondered about what had happened. "Do you know why Crystal climbed the tree?"

"Apparently, she mistook the big, black Newfoundland dog for a bear and panicked." Brody shrugged. "No idea why she thought there were bears around here."

A pit formed in Zach's stomach. He'd implied as much when she'd first come to check out the place, trying to scare her off. His comment that bears seemed to be people's biggest fear was meant to make her think they were in the area. Sure, South Carolina had bears, but up in the mountains, not down by the shore and lake. It hadn't helped he'd also hyped up the fire ants, although they were real. She wouldn't have been in the tree or so panicked without those thoughts. If she had died, it would have been his fault.

"I'm just glad she's safe," Zach said.

"She's lucky you caught her. You sure you're okay?"

"Yeah. Thanks."

Brody turned and took a few steps toward the camp.

"Hey," he called.

Brody paused. "What?"

"Thanks, bro."

After a quick nod, Brody walked back up the slope.

Zach strode to the edge of the lake. He splashed water on his face and took a long, deep breath. The emergency vehicles left, and calming silence filled the space. He stood still for a while, letting his body relax.

He couldn't get Crystal off his mind. She'd been terrified and traumatized. He needed to see if she was okay before he left the area, so he hiked toward her tent.

Chapter Twenty-Five

C rystal crossed her arms and took a deep breath. Light-headed and weak in the legs, she gripped a tent pole for support. She glanced up as Sydney stormed toward her from across the lawn.

"What a complete shit show." Sydney waved her hands, spewing spittle, her face blood-red. "Do you know how much that asshole Zach is costing us?"

"That asshole saved my life."

"Not the point. He ruined an action-packed rescue scene. It would have made a good episode, only we can't use any videos of Zach."

Crystal blinked to clear her vision and fight off the dizziness. "I'd never have approved that clip anyway. You think it was a scene? I wasn't acting. I could have died, but all you care about is this stupid show."

"Damn right. And his interference is delaying our production schedule," Sydney said.

Unbelievable. She admitted she didn't give a crap that Crystal might have died. Her knuckles whitened as she squeezed the pole harder. What kind of person would say such a thing?

Sydney growled, "The next time he meddles, I'm going to sue him and the family for breach of contract."

Oh no. Crystal broke out in a sweat, and her knees quivered. Erin had told Crystal their business was struggling. This park meant everything to that sweet woman and her family. A lawsuit might bankrupt them.

"You've threatened that before. You won't."

"Yes, I will. I'd do it now except there are witnesses to him saving you. He won't be so lucky next time."

Crystal glared at her. "What if I walk off the set?"

"You do and *you'll* be in breach of contract. You can't afford to fight a legal battle or lose this gig."

The muscles in Crystal's neck bunched. It wouldn't help Zach or his brothers if filming stopped. They were counting on the income. She'd have to finish the show.

Sydney took a step closer and wagged a finger in Crystal's face. "I warned Brody and Zach. If he ends up on camera again with you, he'll see us in court."

She stomped toward her car, and Crystal ground her teeth.

Sydney spun wheels out of the lot, kicking up dirt.

Crystal entered the tent, sank to the floor, and sighed.

She glanced at her damp shirt and stained pants. Better dirt than blood. With a shudder, she hugged her knees. That had been too close. She'd never forget the sheer panic of having nothing to grab and falling. If Zach hadn't snatched her from midair, she'd be a lifeless lump at the bottom of the tree.

Footsteps approached. Zach's voice rang out. "Crystal? Just checking to see if you're okay."

She jumped and clasped her hands together. Damn it. What if Sydney was watching?

He'd been warned to stay away. Why was he coming to her tent? Trevor's stationary cameras would catch him on film. Crystal couldn't go out and talk to him. If she told him she'd explain later, they'd hear it and know she planned to see him again.

She had to get him to leave.

Fast.

"Crystal? Answer me. I'm getting worried."

So was she. He wasn't taking Sydney seriously, a big mistake.

Squeezing her eyes shut, Crystal called out, "I'm fine, but I can't talk now. Please leave."

For a long moment, the only sounds came from the forest. Bird calls, leaves rustling, the roar of boats on the lake.

She pressed her lips together and held her breath. Hard as it was, she had to wait this out. It wasn't the time or place to talk with the cameras filming.

At last, she heard the crunch of his retreating footsteps.

When her pounding heart slowed and her tense muscles loosened, she buried her head in her hands and let tears flow. Zach had been heroic, kind, and supportive. When she'd asked him about ever being scared, he'd shared something private. He had no idea how much that meant to her. No wonder he hadn't been excited about them filming on his campgrounds. If he suffered from PTSD, he'd never want the crews, cameras, and chaos.

They'd all overrun his camp today, and now his family's business might be in jeopardy. She had to explain why she'd told him to leave. He deserved a huge apology and a thank you.

In person.

She'd try to catch him at home later. His place wasn't too far, and she'd take her whistle.

No proof it didn't work on bears. Just not on Bear.

She shook her head at the craziness of the whole encounter. That man yelling, "bear," and the big, black animal running toward her. What else was she supposed to think?

Right now, she couldn't think. All she could do was feel, which sucked because she felt like shit. Maybe once she explained to Zach that Sydney was serious about suing his family, he'd understand why Crystal had told him to leave.

The scent of grilled hamburgers drifted into her tent, and her stomach growled. When was the last time she'd eaten? She sure wasn't up for making a fire tonight, so dinner would be an apple and granola bar.

Resting her head against the tent, she closed her eyes and must have drifted off because a voice startled her.

"Hello? It's Mary."

Crystal blinked a couple of times and stood. She unzipped the flap. Mary, holding a foil-covered plate, gazed at her, concern flickering in her eyes. "I heard what happened today and wanted to make sure you were okay."

"Yes. Just tired. But thanks for checking on me."

"Of course." Mary held the plate out. "I figured you'd be too tired to cook, and we have plenty. I hope you can take this?"

Technically, Crystal shouldn't take the food. Too bad. It had been a hell of a day, and she didn't care at this point. "Thank you. I'm starving."

"Remember, we're right next door if you need anything." Mary patted Crystal's arm.

She left and Crystal opened the foil. A cheeseburger and baked beans. Nothing had ever smelled better.

After her attempts at campfire cooking, she'd never take another dinner for granted. Not wanting to look like a total fool, the first meal she'd made had been canned chili and green beans. She'd pulled off heating it up, though, and had even eaten the food.

The panfish was better but still a far cry from the sushi, salads, and grilled seafood she used to be served. It felt like such a distant past, always dining at the best restaurants, attending parties, and celebrity shoots. Yet, everyone just circulated in the crowd, posed for pictures, and nibbled. All a facade.

Here on this island, people were real. They cared. Erin, Mary, Zach, Levi, the list went on. Meanwhile, back in Hollywood, she didn't know a single person who wasn't focused on themselves.

If this show and her influencer status regained her popularity, did she even want to go back there? It was all she'd known, but she was having second thoughts. How happy had she really been, surrounded by people who only cared about being in the limelight? They'd shunned her when her numbers had tanked.

Right now, Crystal had to find a way to make money again, and this was her ticket, so the show must go on.

Footsteps approached, and she stiffened. Please, not Zach again.

"Hey," Angie called.

Great. Still, better than Zach.

Crystal went to the door. "Yeah?"

Angie's gaze flitted over Crystal's clothing. She scoffed. "Guess you didn't post any promos on this outfit today."

"Been busy. What do you want?" Crystal had zero patience at this point for a critique from a rude teenager.

Angie tossed a bag at her. "Mary forgot this. She thinks I'm a delivery service or something. It's from my loser brother. He made brownies."

Crystal's temper snapped. That sweet boy wanted to share his food with her. And this brat insisted on calling her mother Mary? How hurtful.

"I don't know what your problem is, but you're downright mean to your little brother. What did he ever do to you?"

Angie's lips curled. "Exist."

She swung around and tramped back to her camp.

That poor family had their hands full. This day had imploded. Crystal sat on the floor and finished off the meal, her belly satisfied and full.

After a shower, she dressed in pants and a long-sleeved shirt. She hung the whistle over her head and checked her phone. All charged up. She should have plenty of flashlight power to make it to Zach's.

The sun had set, and the woods turned dark. She slipped out of her tent and headed into the forest, her pulse quickening. She stumbled over branches and roots until she was out of camera range.

She swiped on her phone flashlight and stood still, waiting for her eyes to adjust.

Owls hooted, and frogs croaked. Okay. She had this. Nothing harmful. Just the wildlife along the lake. She took one step after another until she found the dirt trail that led to Zach's place.

A rustling came from the woods behind her, and she froze.

Not again.

Three deer stepped onto the dirt path. Their tails flicked, and their ears rotated to catch the slightest sound.

A tiny fawn emerged from the woods and sidled up to the mama on wobbly legs. So small and precious. Crystal stood still. The moon shone on the baby's spotted coat, and its eyes reflected the light from her phone. The deer didn't seem startled, just curious.

She watched until they slipped back into the woods.

Her tight muscles relaxed, and her chest expanded. Such beautiful creatures. Maybe the forest wasn't as scary as Zach made it seem.

At last, she reached his place. The house was lit up, which meant he might be home.

She approached with her flashlight pointed to the ground to avoid tripping. Her heart thumped so fast and loud she was sure he'd hear it from inside.

Chapter Twenty-Six

Z ach took a swig of beer and leaned against the kitchen wall. The sound of Crystal's strangled voice when she'd told him to leave reverberated in his head. After the ordeal they'd been through, she couldn't even come out of the tent to tell him she was all right?

He'd gone out on a limb and shared his deepest secret with her. He scoffed at the literal thought because he had been standing on a branch mere hours ago, spilling his guts. Damn it, he'd let her in. She'd pierced a hole in his shield and then dismissed him. Time to put his armor back on. He'd let himself get too close to her. They had no future together, and he needed his campground back.

A beam of light flashed in the woods. Someone was approaching. He flipped on the porch light and stepped out. "Who's there?"

"It's me, Crystal."

His stomach vaulted. "What are you doing here?"

"I need to talk to you in private."

She must if she'd come on foot through the woods in the dark as scared as she was of the wild animals.

"All right. Come in."

She entered the house, and he shut the door. He steeled himself before turning to her, reinforcing that protective wall she had a habit of crumbling. Not this time.

He faced her. "You told me to leave, so why are you here?"

She twisted her hands. "I...uh...came to apologize."

"For what?"

"For telling you to go away. I wanted to explain at the time, but I couldn't."

Her sad eyes drew him in despite his best efforts. "You could have told me through the tent whatever you came here to say."

"Not with the microphones recording everything. I needed you to leave quickly. The longer you stood there, the more film they'd have of you on the set and Sydney—"

"Just stop." He walked to the other side of the kitchen and made a slashing motion in the air. "I'm sick of Sydney. She doesn't own my life or run this camp."

"You're wrong about that." Crystal lowered her head. "She threatened to sue your family. If you're seen with me again on camera, she'll lawyer up. I feel terrible you're in this mess, when all you've done is try to help me."

She wrapped her arms around herself and rocked on her heels.

So that's why she'd dismissed him. She'd had his family's best interests in mind when she'd told him to leave. His anger deflated like a popped balloon, easing the tension in his rigid body.

"I appreciate everything you've done for me. I'm sorry the company picked this place to film, uprooting your life." She fingered the cuff of her sleeve. "You deserve to have your peaceful world back. I promise I'm going to get them the film they need as fast as possible so we are out of here. I'll leave you alone now."

She took a step toward the door.

"Hold on." He hadn't been prepared for the heartfelt apology and needed a few minutes to process everything she'd told him. "Please sit."

He pulled out the wooden chair at the small kitchen table, and her gaze darted to the door, like she'd rather leave.

"Please," he said again.

She sat under a bright light on a hard chair, her back rigid. Might as well have been an interrogation room.

He opened the refrigerator and pulled out a half-full bottle of wine. "You want a glass? I keep this for my mother. Looks like you could use a drink, though."

Crystal sighed. "Yeah, why not?"

He filled the only wine glass he owned and picked up his beer. "Let's sit over there." He gestured to the loveseat. "It's more comfortable."

She hesitated, but stood and followed him, taking the glass. "Thank you."

When they sat, her leg pressed against his, and warmth spread up his thigh. He shifted to make more space, when all he really wanted was to move closer. And that bothered him. "Helluva day."

"Tell me about it." She tipped the glass and took a swallow.

He glanced at her whistle. "It's my turn to apologize."

"For what?"

"Scaring you about bears. Isn't that why you've been blowing a whistle and climbed the tree?"

"Well, yes. You told me that's what people feared the most, and Angie said one had been spotted in South Carolina. I read the sound of a whistle scares them."

Guilt clawed at his jugular, along with annoyance that the troubled teen had added fuel to the fire. Her parents were regulars, and he'd seen their interactions with Angie over the last two years. She needed help, but that was beside the point right now.

He took another pull of beer and set the can on a tackle box that doubled as a side table. "That bear sighting was up in the mountains. It's rare to see any in this area. I'm sorry for misleading you about them."

Crystal sipped more wine and shook her head. "So you were trying to scare us off?"

"Yeah, and I thought it worked. I was shocked when you came back."

"I didn't really have much choice." She traced a finger down the side of the wineglass.

"Why?"

He studied her face as she drew her mouth to one side like she was deciding whether to say anymore.

At last, she turned to him. "I'm out of money. Close to bankrupt."

And just like that, she'd shared something embarrassing with *him*.

He hadn't seen that coming. Figured she had a ton of money and *Celebrity Trials* was a publicity gig. It made more sense if she needed the show, because she sure as hell wasn't enjoying camping. What had happened to all her money?

"It's my fault." She shrugged. "I trusted people. As a child star, I wasn't legally allowed to make money decisions. I never paid attention to my finances. I've always had other people managing the funds."

"Did they make bad investments for you?" he asked.

Crystal snorted. "If only. No, my mother blew all my earnings. I didn't know it until my credit card was declined, and I started getting overdue notices. By then, it was too late. I should have taken her name off everything long ago, or at least checked my balances."

Holy shit, her own mother? His heart wrenched at the betrayal Crystal must have felt. He pushed to his feet and paced the room, needing to burn off the fury he had for such a despicable parent. "Unbelievable."

"Yup. She's a real piece of work." Crystal finished the rest of her wine.

He took the glass and placed it next to his beer can, then sat back down. "Do you have any recourse?"

"Not really. She spent it all on drugs, no doubt. I don't even know where she is now. She disappeared after the bank account ran dry."

"That sucks." He shook his head. His mom would give up everything she had for any one of her kids.

"I'm sorry." He placed a hand on her leg. Somehow, it felt right there. "Bad enough you had no siblings or even a father. Did anyone have your back?"

She nibbled her lower lip and gave a tiny shake of her head.

Zach's lungs constricted. She had no idea what it was like to have a family to count on for help, or anyone, for that matter. "You're a real trooper. It's amazing how you turned out, considering your upbringing."

She cocked her head and blinked. "What do you mean? I have no savings, my numbers tanked, and I'm relegated to this low-budget reality show. A total failure."

Of course, she'd equate her worth with being popular and accepted by the Hollywood crowd. What else had she known?

"Not true. Growing up in that environment, you could have become an addict or thief. Instead, you made a success of yourself. That's something to be proud of. And you're working hard to get back on top."

"I am, but there's a lot of people out there who still think I'm a loser."

"You aren't defined by the number of likes on social media, and those people don't matter." He squeezed her leg. "There's way more to you."

She gazed at him, the yellow specks in her eyes flickering, like a light shone from within. What was she thinking? She'd gone so still.

"Thanks for saying that." She turned her head.

"You okay?"

"Yeah. It's you I'm worried about. How do you manage to be strong all the time? You saved my life today in the middle of total chaos." She slid her hand on top of his. "That had to be hard. I don't mean to pry, but is it anything you can talk about?"

Her gentle touch spurred emotions he couldn't afford. She had an inflated idea of who he was, and he had to shut that down because they'd never have a relationship. She'd be back on the West Coast soon and out of his life. He needed to make sure she didn't harbor any hero worship or even think about him once she returned.

"I'm not strong all the time. Far from it. Every day is a struggle to keep my shit together." He withdrew his hand and rubbed his tattoo. "This is the date I watched my best friend die. We were sweeping for IEDs. It could easily have been me. Not a day of my life goes by I'm not haunted by the memory, and I can't always control my reactions to it."

"I'm so sorry." Crystal's eyes watered, and she brought a hand to her mouth.

Great, now she pitied him. That's the last thing he wanted.

He stood and strode to the window. Nothing to see out there, but he needed a moment. He hated to be the one who put that look on her face. She deserved someone who made her laugh and enjoy life.

Time spent with him was wasting hers. He had to cut the wire before it detonated.

He gripped the windowsill. "I'm not a hero. Just a messed-up guy who will never live a normal life again. I have nothing to offer anyone. Trust me, if you ever saw one of my breakdowns, you'd run away just like..."

Damn it. He's said too much. His knuckles turned white as he tightened his grip.

"Like who?"

Chapter Twenty-Seven

How could Zach ever think he had nothing to offer anyone? Crystal waited for him to answer her question, a million thoughts whirling in her head. The last one being who had left him because of his PTSD? With his back to her, she couldn't see his face.

The muscles over his shoulder blades bulged, the tension in his body visible. "It doesn't matter who. The bottom line is still the same. Please take me down from the pedestal you put me on. I don't belong there."

Her soul cried for the loss of his best friend and the pain he lived with every day. He was wrong about not being a hero. If only he could see himself through her eyes.

She wanted to say something to make him understand, but words wouldn't come. Hell, she was still reeling from when he'd said, "There's more to you."

He didn't care if she was broke, unpopular, and doing a shitty reality show. None of the things everyone else in her world valued even mattered to him. He cared about *her*, the real her, not the Hollywood version created for publicity and branding. What was she going to do now?

She'd fallen in love with him.

Her heart jolted as the realization hit home.

When? She couldn't say.

When he'd taken her to the urgent care for her poison ivy? When he'd kissed her senseless even with a rash on her face? When he'd taught her to fish? When he'd climbed that tree, despite his anxiety, and caught her, saving her life?

He had it all wrong. She wasn't worthy of *him*.

Every time she'd pushed him away, he'd come back and captured another piece of her heart until he owned it all.

Crazy as it sounded, she'd started thinking about a way to make things work without going back to Hollywood. She needed to share her ideas with Zach.

A glimmer of hope flickered inside. Maybe, just maybe, she could turn her life around and not need to be back in the fray where people didn't give a shit whether she lived or died.

This selfless man did.

If she told him how she felt, he might freak out. She had to take a risk and show him.

She swallowed and took a step closer to him. If he had any feelings for her, she'd find out soon enough.

Pulse racing, she took another step and wrapped her arms around him from behind.

He froze.

"Crystal, what are you doing?"

She took the leap, rested her forehead on his back, and ran her hands over his pecs, feeling them quiver under her touch. "Stop trying to scare me off. It won't work."

His pulse thumped under her fingers. That had to mean something.

"You had it right before. We need to stay away from each other," he said in a strained voice.

"Only from the cameras." She hugged him tighter, pressing her body against him. The heat coming off him lit a fire inside her.

He spun around and held her at arm's length. "You need to go. Don't start this."

His eyes blazed, denying his words.

God help her, she wanted him. From the top of her head to the tips of her toes, and every place between, she *wanted* him. No one had ever made her feel this way. She hadn't believed in love until now. Never thought she'd have sex with someone she loved. But she was all in. No matter what happened down the road, she'd have this moment and this memory, if he'd give it to her.

She reached out, slid her hands down his arms, laced her fingers through his, and stepped closer.

He stood stock-still but his gaze went to her lips. "I'm warning you to stop before I can't."

That sent a chill through her body. He did want her. It was all the encouragement she needed. She wrapped her arms around his neck and kissed him.

For the briefest moment he hesitated, but then kissed her back with a ferocity that sent her senses spinning.

She opened her mouth and was thrilled to the feel of his tongue mating with hers. His fresh, unique scent tantalized her. He unleashed a passion hot and furious in her that now demanded more. *Needed* more.

"Bedroom." He tugged her hand, and she followed.

Standing by the bed, she yanked at his T-shirt, and he flipped it off.

Her eyes devoured his perfectly sculpted torso. She hungered for more, and he brought it.

He trailed blazing kisses along her collarbone, the stubble on his chin tickling and teasing her skin. She threw her head back. His hot breath electrified every nerve in her neck before he brought his mouth back to kiss her again.

She couldn't keep up. The pace, the emotions, the absolute craving she had for him.

He fumbled with the buttons on her blouse.

Liquid fire burned through her, making her bold. She whipped the shirt over her head, along with her bra, in one swift motion. What had he done to her? She was fearless, reckless, and consumed.

Next came the pants. They both struggled to get them off, until they were finally naked, skin to skin. She stood on her tiptoes and kissed him open-mouthed and eager, sliding her breasts against the coarse hair on his chest. The friction titillated her already sensitive nipples.

A low growl rumbled from deep inside, and his mouth stole her breath as he grabbed her ass, pinning her to him. His hard cock pressed against her stomach, and she reached down.

He caught her hand and shook his head. "Don't. If you touch me, I won't last."

His plea sent another spike of heat to her core. The temptation to take him over the top was real, but he swept her into another realm before she had time to think about it. Not that she could think much at all with him doing such magical things to her body.

He palmed her breasts. "So beautiful."

Edging her to sit on the bed, he dropped to his knees. He flicked a finger at a nipple, then took it into his mouth.

She sucked in a breath as his hands grazed her sides and he inched one up to her sex, tickling her nub with a finger.

She'd never been so stimulated. No one had ever touched her like this, and her body flamed. She kneaded his shoulders as he continued to torture her nipple, sliding a finger inside of her.

Her body quaked as the muscles tightened, begging for release. This was all Zach. Just knowing it was him touching her, making her crazy with need, drove her fast to the edge.

He circled her clit with his thumb and suckled her breast. Her hard nipple tingled against the rasp of his tongue.

A wave of ecstasy rose, building and building.

Her thighs trembled.

She fisted a hand in his hair and held on, crying out as she shattered into beautiful bliss, her body shuddering while she clung to him. "Now, Zach. I want to feel you inside me."

With a groan, he stepped back. "Don't move. I have to find a condom."

He disappeared into the bathroom and came out a few seconds later holding one. He rolled it down his hard length. She watched, more aroused than ever, and a little scared. She was going to do this for the first time. But it was Zach, and she loved him.

Rising from the bed, she kissed him hard, nipping his lower lip with her teeth. Like lightning, desire bolted through her again. "I want you so much."

"Back at you." He eased her onto the bed.

She gazed up at him.

His pupils were dark and dilated. The muscles in his arms bulged as he held his body above hers, his face taut. It exhilarated her to know she brought him to this intense state. He wanted her as much as she wanted him.

She raised her hips, and he slid the tip of his cock inside of her. In and out, just the tip. Teasing and tormenting, causing another wave of rapture to build.

The nerves at her sex begged for release. She gripped his shoulders, digging her nails into the firm flesh over his strained muscles. "More, Zach, more."

"I can't wait any longer," he said in a tortured voice and then thrust deep inside of her.

She gasped at a sharp pain.

He stilled, and the whites of his eyes flashed. "Holy shit. Are you...this can't be—"

Chapter Twenty-Eight

S he was a virgin.

"Don't stop." Crystal tugged his shoulders.

Zach froze, shocked. Who would ever have thought that, and why on earth was she giving it to him? He didn't deserve it. But at this point, the damage was done, and even though his raging hard-on screamed for release, he cared more about her than satisfying the need. "I don't want to hurt you."

She shook her head hard. "No, the pain passed. Now I just... need you. Please."

Her eyes begged him, and she rocked her hips, flicking her tongue out before biting her lip.

Watching her teeth nip that plump lower lip drove him insane. He covered her mouth with his and gently slid his cock in and out. She was so wet and tight. Each movement caused a pulse to travel the length of his dick, and he fought for control. Now that he knew, he didn't want to take things too fast.

She kissed him, her tongue probing with wild abandon, while her hips matched his rhythm. Heat rose from their joined bodies, and her scent filled his nostrils. A sheen of sweat formed between them as he picked up the pace.

Moaning into his mouth, she clung to him and trembled. Her

thighs tightened, and she dug her nails into his back. Knowing she was close to coming again sent a thrill through him and brought him nearly to the brink.

He broke the kiss to gaze at her, wanting to see what she looked like in the heat of passion.

Desire burned in her darkened eyes.

Heightened by excitement, her red cheeks flamed as she strained against him, eager to meet each thrust. Her blond hair was splayed out on the pillow. *His* pillow, on *his* bed. He took primal satisfaction in that for reasons he wouldn't think about right now. His body had taken control of his brain.

"Faster. Harder," she demanded in a strung-out voice.

God, she was incredible. This was incredible. Sex had never been like this before. He was consumed by her. Her scent, the way her swollen lips parted as she panted and gasped for air, staring up at him like her very soul was searing into his.

Her tiny whimpers called to his heart. Hard to hear with the blood roaring in his ears. Like whitewater rapids headed toward a waterfall, his body surged to the precipice. Each plunge into her building more pressure. He wouldn't last much longer.

She threw her head back, arched up, and dug her nails deeper. "Oh...God...Zach," she cried out.

Hearing her call out his name and feeling the walls of her throbbing around his cock catapulted him over the edge.

With a final, hard thrust, he exploded with a deep growl. An orgasm ripped through him with pulsating, heat-searing, mindblowing intensity like never before. The sensation went on and on until, at last, out of breath, his lungs sucked in air.

Good God.

He shuddered as each aftershock hit, making his dick twinge.

She went limp beneath him, also quaking.

He pulled out of her and rolled to his side, breathing heavy.

The sound of them both gasping for air filled the room. He closed his eyes, recovering, and warring with his emotions as a million thoughts vied for his attention.

He'd hurt her. Thrust into her like some caveman, but damn it, he hadn't known. Why hadn't she told him? And why him?

That was the kicker. She must have had opportunities, and yet she'd waited and held out for him? He felt unworthy. In a few weeks, she'd be gone and never see him again.

She slung an arm across his stomach, snuggled next to him, and rested her head on his shoulder. "That was...I don't have words. Is it always like that?"

He squeezed her hand. "No. That was intense."

"In a good way, right?" she asked in a soft, shaky voice.

Hell, yeah. As in earth-shattering. He rubbed his thumb on her knuckle. "The best it's ever been for me."

Her warm breasts pressed against his side, and the tease of her breath over his chest stirred him. Oh no, he wasn't going to start back up again.

They needed to talk about what had just happened because he didn't understand.

He kissed the top of her head. "Do you want to use the restroom before I take care of things?"

She gave a quick nod and disappeared into the bathroom. While he waited for her in bed, he ticked through the questions swirling in his head. What now? This was all new territory. It wasn't like he'd been celibate. He'd had some hook-ups after coming back stateside, but they'd been casual sex, and not recent. Hell, he'd even had trouble finding the condoms. The dry spell wasn't the issue, though. Nothing he'd ever experienced came even close to what he'd felt with Crystal, and that scared the shit out of him.

She returned, slid onto the bed, and quickly pulled the sheet up. Was she embarrassed at being naked? As beautiful as she was, she shouldn't be. Then again, she'd never done this before.

"Gimme a sec, and I'll be right back." He patted her shoulder.

After doing what he needed, he splashed some water on his face, took a deep breath, and went back to the bedroom.

Crystal was curled up, her head resting on his pillow, eyes wide. The picture of vulnerability.

He slipped onto the bed, and she snuggled up against him. Damn if her curves didn't fit right into his side, and the feel of her silky hair on his shoulder made him want to hit replay. But no. That wasn't happening. Deeper emotions pulsed through him.

"I think we should talk about this." His throat tightened, still dealing with the fact she'd been a virgin.

She brushed her hair back and raised her head to meet his eyes. "Okay."

Shit, he hated to see that look, like she was afraid of what he might say next.

He touched her cheek. "I don't understand. Why did you decide to do this with me? If you waited this long, it makes me think you were holding out for the right person."

She lowered her head and shrugged before peering back up at him, her blue eyes shining with hope. "What if *you* are that person?"

Whoa. His heart hit the brakes, skidding to a halt.

"I mean, I've been thinking about it, I might not have to go back to Hollywood." She tucked her hair behind an ear. "I have other options. I—"

"Wait." He ran a hand down his face.

He had to stop that train of thought in its tracks. He'd told her about the PTSD. Even if he wanted to be the right person, he couldn't give her what she needed. She deserved to be with someone who'd make her happy.

"I don't think you understand how bad things can get with me. I can't subject you to that."

"I'm not worried. I'll handle whatever happens. You don't scare me. I've seen how you care about people." She shook her head and gazed into his eyes. "You took me to the doctor when I got poison ivy. You gave up your house to me and even bought an air conditioner. You taught me how to fish."

"Crystal, stop. You don't know how—"

"Shh." She put a finger to his lips. "I'm not done. The list goes on. Your devotion to your mother, your concern for my safety. My point is, I...I want to try to be with you if you have feelings for me."

A tight band cinched his ribs, making it hard to breathe. He'd reached the point of emotional overload and didn't know how to handle this outpouring.

"I do care about you, which is why I can't burden you with my baggage."

Her eyes turned glassy. "If I want to take that on, it's my choice."

Overwhelmed with what she'd just told him and what she was willing to give up for him, he was at a loss for words. "I don't know what to say."

"Neither do I. Maybe we can think about it?"

Think about it? Yeah, he could think about it. He could dream about it. He could imagine what it would be like to be with her every day. But at the risk of hurting her because she didn't know what she was signing up for? That wasn't in his DNA.

"All right. We can think on it," he said.

She rubbed her eyes. "I'm tired, and I can't focus anymore. Can we talk about this another time?"

"Yes." It would give him a chance to process everything she'd told him and keep him from saying anything hurtful. "I should take you back, unless you want to stay for a while and get a little sleep? I'd like that." He cupped her cheek and kissed her.

"So would I." She slunk down and rested her head on his shoulder.

He couldn't promise her the future, but he'd take this one night together. An unbearable ache formed in his chest at the thought of not being the man she needed, and having to let her go.

Her breathing became steady, and her body softened against him. Closing his eyes, he surrendered to the physical and mental fatigue of the day.

Crystal shifted in his arms, and Zach blinked, glancing at the alarm clock. Five o'clock. He must have fallen asleep.

His breath caught. When was the last time he'd slept until morning with no nightmares? Not a single night came to mind since he'd been back.

His thoughts went to Crystal, who'd slung a leg over his thighs and rested a hand on his torso. Her warm body molded to his brought back memories of the night before. The incredible sex followed by the things she'd said to him.

Except for his reaction to the chaos yesterday, he'd had fewer incidents since she'd come to the island. Now he'd slept uninterrupted all night.

A glimmer of hope lit inside. Of course, she hadn't cured him, but what if being around her helped? Maybe there *was* a way for them to be together without him scaring her. He'd be lying to himself if he didn't admit she'd brought light to his life. For the first time in years, he felt alive. Not hunkered down in the woods, isolated. She, too, had been thrown into a tough situation, yet she had spunk and attitude in spades.

What mattered the most, though, was whether he could make *her* happy. He flashed back to the different ways her eyes sparkled. She had several. The mischievous way, when he'd told her about the pranks he and Levi played on each other growing up. The grateful way, when he'd brought her to the urgent care. The playful way, when she'd put on that silly hat at his mom's and asked if he liked it.

"Mmm." She moved against his side, her soft skin caressing him.

His cock twinged.

Trouble.

He had to get her back to the camp before the sun came up. But he couldn't tear his gaze from her sweet face, so peaceful and innocent in slumber. He squeezed her. "I'm sorry to wake you. It's time to take you back."

She slid her leg off him and sat up. Yawning, she shook her head. "Wait, you can't, the cameras will—"

"It's okay. I'll drop you at the perimeter, out of their range, and watch from there to make sure you get back safe."

"All right. Thanks."

He eyed her. Even with tousled hair, a pink cheek from where she'd rested against him, and sleepy eyes, she was still gorgeous. More so than when she was glammed up because this was the natural and real side of her. What would it be like to wake up to that every morning?

She took a deep breath and placed her palm on his forearm. "Can we finish our conversation from last night? You admitted you have feelings for me."

"I do."

"I meant what I said about wanting to be with you. You don't get to decide what I need or what risks I should take." She shook her head. "I'm done with that in my life. Other people have controlled things for too long. It's what landed me here. At least from now on, the mistakes I make will be my own. And for the record, I don't think this is one."

This was going to be tough. Despite his earlier thoughts about wanting to make her happy, his protective instincts ran deep. He'd been taught and trained to be the risk taker to ensure no one got hurt. The weight of that responsibility sat on his shoulders. His battle scars shouldn't be her problem. Still, she made a good point. How would he feel if someone took away *his* free will to make life choices?

"Hear me out. I've given this some thought." She tapped the side of her head. "Your business could grow with some savvy marketing. I can use my social media platforms and influencer status to promote the park. Also, your mother wants to pursue the wedding venue idea I'd mentioned. She said she wished she could hire me to help. I wouldn't need to go back to California if I did either or both of these."

Wow. Zach let the words sink in, feeling a bit blindsided that she'd been thinking about a possible future together, and he'd had no idea.

She shrugged. "If nothing else, I'm making money as an influencer, and I'm confident I can find another company that would want my marketing skills. It wouldn't even have to be local with technology these days."

Zach's heart surged against his rib cage, too full to be contained. Not only had she given a special part of herself to him, she was willing to make huge changes for a chance to be with him. She'd thought it all through, which meant this wasn't an emotional response from having sex with him. It humbled and terrified him at the same time because he wanted it so much, but at what cost to her?

Chapter Twenty-Nine

Crystal held her breath after baring her soul to Zach. His silence and set jaw told her he was battling with what to say, which might be good or bad. Her pulse thinned as she waited, hoping he'd take the leap and give them a chance together.

What they'd shared had been nothing short of amazing. She'd had no idea what sex could be like. Something told her it wasn't this way for everyone. He'd said it had been the best ever for him, and she wasn't even experienced enough to know what to do. Could it get even better? At the end of the day, that wasn't what was important. Their future together was all she cared about.

She blinked and refocused on his face. What mattered now was what he said next, because if he shut her down, it was over.

Taking her hand, he swallowed. "There's no logic to us trying to be together. We're complete opposites and have totally different lifestyles."

Her hope dropped like ratings after a tanked show. He was right. But what she felt for him had nothing to do with logic. Lowering her head, she fought back tears. She wouldn't beg him. If he didn't feel the same way about her, then she had to move on and try to forget about him. Like that would ever happen.

He cleared his throat. "The thing is..."

She jerked her head back up.

His eyes softened, and he stroked her hand. "I don't understand how it would work, and I can't make any promises, but..."

Her lungs caved as she hung on to his every word. "But?"

Straightening his shoulders, he let out a breath and said, "Maybe we can give it a shot?"

This time she didn't fight back the tears. Her eyes welled, and she threw her arms around him, crushing him with a hug.

He kissed her head and stroked her back. "Let's take it one day at a time and try to figure things out."

She nodded into his shoulder, too choked up to speak.

"You're worth it," he whispered into her ear.

Her soul leaped for joy at the words she thought she'd never hear or believe. He gave her hope, and she'd do everything in her power to make him happy.

Crystal unzipped her tent and stepped outside. Almost seven at night and still hot as hell. Zach hadn't been around since he'd dropped her off earlier that morning. She knew he needed to stay away from her camp, but it was killing her not to see him. What if he'd changed his mind about giving them a chance? She broke out in a sweat.

All day she'd thought about him while working the kayak scene they never filmed after the bear fiasco yesterday. Sydney seemed happy to have more footage and mentioned they were nearly done. It made no sense, though, because of all the scenes they'd have to cut that Crystal wouldn't approve. Whatever. The producers had to know how much film they needed.

The sound of jingling dog tags came from the camp next door. Angie stood by the tent while Murphy sniffed the ground. Of course, he was soaking wet again from swimming in the lake. Maybe he'd stay over there for a change.

Crystal sighed and sat on a rock by the edge of the campfire. What was she going to do now? Her blog had taken off, and she had several ideas for how to make money, but they all needed to be worked out. Was she willing to change her entire life to be with Zach? Could she handle being in the sticks after all her time in Hollywood?

Shutting her eyes, she flashed back to the way he'd made her feel last night. It wasn't just about the sex. He'd given all of himself to her. Everything about the man was *real* and solid. She trusted him, something that didn't come easy for her. He had no agenda or need to use her. She shifted, feeling a bit achy in parts she wasn't used to, but in a good way. A reminder of what they'd shared and would again with any hope.

She stood and dusted off her pants. Maybe a walk by the water would help clear her head. Something about being by the sparkling lake and feeling the sun on her face soothed her. Yeah, she *could* get used to being in nature.

She took a step into the brush. A rattle sounded, and she froze. A coiled rattlesnake sat in a hollow under a tree.

She screeched, trying to back up.

Panicked, feet scrambling, she kicked up dust and leaves at the snake as she fell on her butt.

The snake's tail rattled harder, and it coiled tighter.

She was only a foot from it, well within striking distance.

Oh no, oh no, oh no.

Her heart raced triple-time as she tried to ease away in a crab-walk.

Murphy bounded down the hill barking. Just as the snake struck, he lunged at it.

The snake bit him right in the mouth.

Murphy whelped and tried to attack again, but the snake streaked off into the woods.

A flood of adrenaline shot Crystal to her feet as the dog flopped down, panting.

Angie raced up to them and dropped to her knees. "Oh my

God. Murphy! He...he...his tongue is bleeding. That snake bit his tongue."

Crystal's pulse ran a fast track through her body, and she forced herself to focus. Murphy might have saved her life. Thank God she'd read the section on snakes in Zach's endless safety manual. Although that hadn't done her any good when she'd freaked out instead of moving slowly. Her fault Murphy had taken the hit. She'd make it up to him.

"We have to get him to a vet. Where are your parents?"

Angie shook her head hard. "They're fishing way far out on the lake. I was supposed to take care of him." She hugged him, tears streaming down her face. "Don't die. Don't die."

Shit. Crystal had to act fast. "Angie, let go of him so he can breathe. We need to keep him calm. Look at me."

The girl released her hold and bobbed her head. "Okay. What do we do?"

"I'll call for help." When Crystal tried to reach Zach, the call went right to voicemail.

Double shit. Murphy panted harder, and his tongue was bleeding more.

Crystal glanced up the hill to their car. "Are the keys to that here?"

"Yeah, I know where they are."

Great. If she drove him to the vet, it would save time calling around trying to find someone else to help. "Call your parents and grab the keys. Ask if I can use the car to take him to the vet."

"Got it." Angie raced up the hill, and Crystal ran into the tent and grabbed a bottle of water. She doused Murphy's tongue with it and steeled her back. She had this. No way this dog was going to die after saving her life.

Angie came back breathless, clutching the keys. "You can use our car. They're heading back and said not to wait."

"Okay." Crystal forced a deep breath. "Stay with him and listen to me."

"Wh-what?"

"You have a job, and it's to remain calm. If he thinks you're upset, things will be harder for him. Can you sing him a song or something?"

"Sing?" Angie's eyes clouded, then cleared, shining bright. "Yeah, I can sing. I mean, I haven't for a long time, but yes, I can."

Crystal ran to the car, shocked to hear Angie singing in a beautiful, sweet voice to the dog she'd only pretended not to love.

Every second mattered with a rattlesnake bite, and Crystal's fingers shook as she searched on her phone for an emergency vet clinic. The closest one was thirty minutes away. That was pushing the time limit on getting the shot, but it's all she could hope for after hours. Between her and Angie, they hauled Murphy into the car.

Angie sat in the back with him, still singing sweetly and stroking his head.

"I need you to call the clinic and let them know we're coming with a rattlesnake bite injury to a dog. Can you please do that?" Crystal asked.

"Um...Yes. What's the number?"

"I'm using the GPS on my phone. Can you look it up on yours?"

"I'm scared. I don't—"

"Angie?" Crystal glanced in the rearview mirror.

"Yeah?"

"We're in this together. Remember, no freaking out. Search for Meyer's Animal Hospital. It should be about a half hour from here."

"Right." Angie's head dipped and a second later she said, "I got it."

Crystal nodded. "Great. Give them a call."

Twenty-five minutes and counting to the center. He had to be okay. She couldn't see him from the back seat, but his labored breathing tore at her heart. How had she ever cared that the dog had shaken water on her? Like so many things in life, she'd been in a bubble, never seeing how much people and even dogs loved each other.

"I...umm...my dog might be dying...we're on the way..."

Good God, the clinic would have no idea what to prepare for with Angie's description. Poor girl was an emotional mess. Who could blame her? When had Crystal ever had to deal with something this important? Huh, maybe just now. "Put on speaker phone, please."

"Okay. I'll hold the phone closer to you."

"Hello? Can you hear me?" Crystal called out.

"Yes. How can I help you?"

"I'm bringing a dog in that has been bitten on the tongue by a rattlesnake, and I wanted to give you a heads up. We should be there in about twenty minutes," Crystal said.

"Thanks for the information. We'll be ready for you. I'm sorry, but anti-venom is expensive, and I'll need a pre-payment before we can treat him. Will you be able to take care of that?"

Crystal's knuckles whitened on the steering wheel. She had one card with a small credit limit. She prayed it would be enough.

Angie's desperate gaze darted to hers in the rear-view mirror.

"If I don't have enough credit left on my card, can I make arrangements to pay it off?" Crystal asked.

Silence on the other end.

"My parents will pay when they get there," Angie said, her voice breaking.

Crystal held her breath. The woman had said they needed the money before they gave him the shot, and time was critical.

"Just come in, and we'll see what we have to work with," the receptionist said.

"Okay. Thank you." She gripped the wheel tighter, unsure how much she could cover on a low limit credit card that already had some charges. Somehow, she'd figure it out. And if Angie's parents ended up paying the balance, Crystal would make sure to reimburse them. This was all on her. The dog had saved her life.

"He's drooling now," Angie's voice rose from the back seat.

Crystal kept her eyes on the road, her mind shifting back to how Zach had talked to her when she'd been panicked in the tree and nervous at the urgent care. The man deserved a medal.

Even though he had his issues, he'd calmed her down by talking and distracting her. That's what she needed to do for Angie, because if she kept panicking, Murphy's blood pressure would zoom venom through his system and make him worse.

"This is a normal reaction for a dog with a snakebite. That's why we're going to the clinic. It's treatable, and he's a big boy. He'll be fine." Crystal hoped her words sounded more reassuring than her scary thoughts. "You have an incredible voice. Have you ever considered the arts at school?"

"I, umm...wait, are you sure he's going to be okay? He doesn't look good."

Crystal drew upon her acting skills to keep her voice light. "Yes. I read about this. It's textbook, and we'll make it there in time. So, what about the arts?"

Angie shrugged. "It's not cool to be in theater."

"Really? Do you think I'm not cool?"

"You? No. You're like, famous and stuff. Well, you used to be."

That stung, but sometimes the truth hurt. Her phone beeped and a banner came across the top. Zach was calling. Her stomach jumped. She couldn't turn off the GPS and wasn't about to have a speaker phone conversation in front of Angie. She'd have to get back to him after Murphy was admitted.

"The clinic is just up ahead. You stay in the car with him while I let them know we're here. They might want to help get him inside." She pulled into the lot and parked. "Maybe you can sing to him again? I think it soothed him."

Angie swiped at a tear and nodded.

Crystal's blood coursed through her veins as she raced into the building and was greeted by the receptionist.

Two techs hustled out with a stretcher to get Murphy.

Angie followed them in as they hurried the dog to a back room.

"Just one second, I need to speak with the doctor to figure out the fee. We never know until we see the size of the dog and assess its condition." The woman stepped away from the desk.

"I have fifty dollars back at camp." Angie rubbed her arms.

Crystal's heart wrenched. The poor kid had puffy eyes and black mascara smeared down her cheeks. She was even shaking. Without thinking, Crystal wrapped an arm around her and squeezed. "We won't need your money. I'll take care of this."

"But what if—"

"No what ifs. I promise, I got this." She sure sounded confident, if only she felt it. "Why don't you use the restroom and splash some water on your face? It might make you feel better. I'll be right here."

"Yeah, okay." Angie nodded and headed across the room.

Phew.

She didn't want her to be standing there if she had to negotiate with the receptionist.

The woman came back with a printout. "Here are the initial charges that need to be paid prior to treatment. There could be more, but if you can cover this, we'll get started."

Wow. She hadn't been kidding about the expense of the anti-venom. Crystal handed her the credit card.

Her pulse throbbed in her veins, and she dug her nails into her palm as the woman swiped the card.

Agonizing seconds ticked by until the machine beeped.

"It went through." The receptionist tore off the receipt. "If you can sign this, I'll let the doctor know we have the green light."

Crystal let out an audible breath and picked up the pen with a shaky hand. Thank God, they could at least give him the shot. She'd take it one step at a time.

Angie returned, her face pink from scrubbing makeup and tears from her cheeks.

"Everything is paid up for now. Don't worry, they're treating him. Why don't you sit down and try to relax? I need to make a call," she said.

She stepped outside and dialed Zach.

He picked up on the first ring. "Where are you?"

The sound of his voice sent a thrill through her body. God, it was good to hear from him. "We're at Meyer's Animal Hospital. I needed the GPS and couldn't answer the phone earlier."

"It's okay. Paul called me from the boat and said Murphy got bit by a rattlesnake. He asked for a ride, so I'm picking up the family from the dock to bring them. At least I know where to go now. What happened? They didn't have details."

"He's being treated. I don't know much else about his health yet. I'll fill you in on the rest when you get here. Angie is a wreck, and I need to get back to her."

"All right. See you soon."

She hung up and took a seat next to Angie. "Zach's bringing your family once they meet him at the dock."

"Okay." She frowned at her phone screen. "This says a lot of dogs die from rattlesnake bites."

"The internet can be scary. People always post the worst stories, and you never know which sites to trust. Murphy is being cared for and should be okay. We got him here fast."

Crystal covered the screen with her palm. "You know I made it to the top without much talent. With that voice of yours, you might have a shot."

Angie rolled her eyes. "Now you sound like my mom. She keeps saying the same thing."

"Maybe you should listen to her. She's in your corner. Trust me, I know the difference."

"What do you mean?"

Her shoulders tensed. If she had any chance of getting through to the kid, she might need to share some of her painful past. "My mother only used me to make money. She never cared about me. I'm sure your parents want you to be happy and to share your gift. I'd have given anything for that kind of love and support. Maybe cut them some slack?"

Angie frowned. "You mean you grew up with no family?"

"Yup."

"So you never went to any birthday parties for relatives? Barbecues in the backyard with balloons everywhere?"

Celebrating birthdays? Crystal's mother was never sober enough to remember one. "No, and that's my point. Don't take it for granted. Those people will be there for you."

Angie studied her shoes and blinked a few times.

Crystal could only hope she'd reached her.

The receptionist rounded the desk and approached them.

Crystal and Angie sprang to their feet.

The woman smiled. "I have good news. Murphy is responding to the shot and is well on his way to recovery."

"Oh, thank God," Crystal said.

"We need to keep an eye on him for a while, but we expect he'll be fine."

"Thank you for saving Murphy." Angie hugged Crystal.

Tears stung her eyes as she hugged her back. "You have it wrong. He saved me."

When she let go, Angie stepped back and rubbed her arms again. Poor kid must feel awkward, unused to showing affection.

They both plopped down in the chairs, heaving a sigh.

"Text your parents to let them know Murphy's going to be okay, and I'll tell Zach." She shot a quick message off to him. He might not see it since he was driving, but Mary or Paul would probably tell him.

Angie typed on her phone and settled back in the chair. She glanced at Crystal. "You can't think you don't have talent. Look at how popular your blog is now, and your fashion line is amazing."

"You follow me?" That was a surprise. The girl didn't dress like someone who kept up with the latest trends. More like she combined different ones together, and it didn't work.

"Yeah," she said in a quiet voice as if she was embarrassed. "I mean, I can't wear those kinds of clothes, but I like looking at them."

"Why can't you wear them?"

"Please, I'm not a size zero." Angie turned her head and faced the window.

Crystal's throat constricted as images flashed in her mind of all the photo shoots she'd done. Always under pressure to stay thin and watch every bite she ate. Her old fashion line did lend itself to skinny women. She hadn't even realized what message she'd been sending out while so immersed in the Hollywood lifestyle.

Her new blog was completely different. The camping outfits she showcased came in all sizes, and she'd picked up a whole new audience.

"No one has to be a size zero to feel good about themself. It doesn't matter what anyone else thinks."

Crystal stopped short at the words coming out of her mouth. For her whole life, it had always mattered what other people thought. Since when did she not care about it? Of course, she still wanted followers and good ratings, but for the first time, she was getting them on her own by just being herself. She believed in the products she promoted, and her platform had changed. No more catering to the Hollywood crowd, which suited her fine, because she liked her new supporters. Sometimes change was a good thing.

"Would you be open to trying out a different look?"

"Maybe, but I wouldn't know where to start." Angie fiddled with the hem of her shirt.

"I do. I can already picture an outfit that would make you shine. Gimme a sec." Crystal eyed Angie and went to work on her phone. Satisfied, she held the screen up. "What do you think of this?"

"Wow. That's great. I mean, for sure a new look. I'd wear it, though."

"I bet your mom would take you to the mall and help you pick some clothes out."

Angie bit her lip. "I don't know. She's pretty upset with me these days, and I don't want to rack up bills. She already bought me shorts and a T-shirt from the camp store, and I told her it was a waste of money because I'd never wear them."

Yeah, Mary had a good reason to be distraught because she loved her daughter. And how many teenagers cared about what their family spent on their clothes? Another win in the column of good parenting, even though they were going through a rough patch.

"Clothes don't have to be expensive. There are knock-off stores and thrift shops—"

"Wait a sec." Angie's eyes bulged. "*You* go to thrift shops?"

Crystal shrugged. That was the second time someone had reacted with shock. "I never used to. You can find some decent clothes if you take the time to dig through the racks."

"I'd never know what to look for." Angie frowned.

"You can send me pictures, and I'll help you decide."

"You'd do that for me? Why?"

Good question. A piece of Crystal's heart ached for the little girl she'd been when thrown into the limelight. She knew the loneliness of being different and not fitting in. Angie wanted to be accepted. She sounded like she was ready for a change. Of course, new clothes alone wouldn't be enough. She'd need to step out of her shell, but it would be a good start. "Believe it or not, I can relate to what you're going through. If I can help with a simple thing like this, I'm happy to."

"You're not at all how I thought you'd be." Angie shifted in her chair to face her. "I'm sorry I've treated you like crap the whole time you've been here."

Crystal cocked her head and wrinkled her nose. "I probably was that person when I got here. I've learned a lot more than how to camp since then."

Angelic laughed. "Good, because, no offense, but you kinda suck at the camping stuff."

"Says the pot to the kettle." Crystal grinned and nudged her. She turned at the sound of a vehicle pulling into the parking lot. Her belly somersaulted at the sight of Zach's truck.

Chapter Thirty

P aul, Mary, and Johnny climbed out of Zach's truck in front of the vet hospital. He hurried to open the front door, and followed them inside, eager to see for himself that Crystal was okay. This had to have scared the crap out of her.

Angie sprang out of her chair and launched herself into Mary's arms. "Mom, I'm so sorry. I didn't mean for him to get hurt."

Mary froze. Her eyes widened, and she hugged her sobbing daughter.

"Things like this happen in the woods. It's not your fault." She stroked Angie's back. Mary's eyes filled with tears, and Johnny's lips trembled as he grabbed his dad's hand. "Why's everybody crying? Is Murphy going to die?"

Angie let go of her mother and knelt, placing a hand on Johnny's shoulder. "No. He's fine. I promise. Crystal got him here super-fast, and they said he's doing great."

Paul's jaw dropped, and his eyes turned glassy.

Zach's throat closed a bit as he took in the sight. He'd never seen Angie act so nice to her brother.

Even Crystal was blinking hard now.

"They have a bowl of candy on the desk. You wanna pick out a piece?" Angie smiled at her brother.

He bobbed his head and followed her to the counter.

Bringing a hand to her mouth, Mary leaned against Paul. "What the—"

"You must be Murphy's owners?" a woman called out as she approached from the front.

"Yes," Paul said.

"I'm happy to say he's doing well. We need to keep him a bit longer to make sure, but he's out of the woods."

"That's such great news. We were so worried until my daughter texted us he was going to be okay. I'm sure there's paperwork and a bill to pay. I'll—"

She shook her head. "All taken care of by Ms. Lovechild. There won't be additional charges for us monitoring him since he didn't need any more medication."

Zach's gaze flew to Crystal. She'd told him she was almost bankrupt, and emergency vets were expensive.

Paul stepped closer to Crystal. "We need to pay for this. You already did enough by bringing him here."

"Your dog saved my life. Taking care of the bill is the least I can do."

Paul held his hands out. "Any way I can talk you out of it?"

"Not a chance." Crystal gave a small shake of her head. "I'm just glad it all ended well."

Angie returned with Johnny, who sucked on a lollipop.

Mary's eyes softened as she watched them together. They took a seat in the waiting room.

"I have some release instructions to give you if you'll follow me to the desk," the woman said to Paul.

Mary glanced up at Crystal. "Sounds like it's going to be a while here. I don't want to keep you and Zach any longer." She turned to him. "Would you mind taking Crystal back?"

Mind? Hell no, he wouldn't mind. He wouldn't mind one bit taking her back to his house and doing a repeat of the night before, but she'd need some rest after all this. Didn't mean he couldn't think about it, though. "No problem. I want to hear the whole story, anyway."

"Great. I appreciate you bringing us out here."

Crystal handed Mary the keys to their car. "I hope everything is fine tonight."

"I'm sure it will be. Thanks so much." Mary walked over to the kids and sat beside Johnny.

Zach gazed down at Crystal. Now that the commotion was over, he had a chance to really look at her. He'd been thinking about her all day. The softness of her skin when he'd stroked her body and the fire in her eyes when she'd demanded more. God help him, he craved her like a drug.

Her cheeks pinkened, as a shy smile formed. So, she'd been thinking about him too. And apparently, he *could* make her smile.

"You ready?" He touched her arm, and his heart slid sideways at the mere contact.

"Yeah." She waved to Mary and the kids as she headed toward the door. "I'll see you all back at camp. Good luck with Murphy."

"Hold on." Angie stood and crossed the room, stopping in front of Crystal. "I...uh...I want to tell my mom what you said about the clothes if you still want to help me?"

"Sure." She gave Angie a quick pat on the shoulder. "We'll come up with a plan."

"Thanks." Angie shifted her feet. "For...you know...everything."

"You got it. Catch you later." She grinned and glanced at Mary, who was staring with wide eyes.

Zach opened the door for Crystal. He'd have to ask what that was all about. Something must have gone down between her and Angie because the girl was acting completely different. She'd even been nice to her brother.

When Crystal sank into the passenger seat, he started the engine and placed a hand on her shoulder. "You okay?"

"Yup. Just tired."

"No doubt." He put the truck in gear and pulled out of the parking lot. "Wanna tell me what happened?"

She sighed and nodded. "Murphy attacked a snake when it was about to strike me. I freaked out, which I know is in your book of things-not-to-do."

His belly flipped at the comment, and he hitched an eyebrow. "You read some of it?"

"Uh huh. The parts on snakes, thank God."

"Glad to hear it. There's hope for you yet." He tried to keep things light, but she'd been in real danger. "I'm sorry I didn't answer your call. I was in a patchy service spot, and it never came through."

"It's okay. I figured things out."

"You really did. I can't tell you how impressed I am."

"What do you mean? That dog almost died because of me." She shrunk into the seat.

"Just the opposite." He found a place to park on the side of the road. This needed his full attention. He turned to her. "You took complete control of this. It could have gone south fast."

"Yeah, I know. I was nervous about having enough credit on my card. It was a nail-biter. In the end, I was able to cover the fee."

He rested a hand on her knee. "Like I said, you really managed the situation."

"I still panicked. You know how bad I am in an emergency." She lowered her head.

"But you weren't this time." He squeezed her leg. "You found a way to get to the vet fast, and you must have kept it together or you wouldn't have made it there. That's a major thing. Don't discount it."

"I didn't have a choice. Angie was a mess, and I...channeled you. That's how I got through it."

What was she talking about? "You channeled me?"

"Yeah." She brushed her hair back and shrugged. "You know, like when we were in the tree, and you talked to me? I thought maybe if I talked to Angie, it might calm her. And then I asked her to sing to Murphy. Did you know she has a beautiful voice?"

He shook his head. "No, but I knew something happened

between you two." He cupped her cheek with his hand. "You have no idea how special you are."

"You're making too much of all this." She squirmed.

"I don't think so. I saw Angie acting nice to her family. It was nothing short of a miracle. What did you say to her?"

"Eh, we just talked about fashion and stuff."

"Why are you brushing this off when you deserve some credit here?"

She frowned. "I don't know. I shared some things with her that are kind of hard to talk about for me."

Now it made sense. She must have discussed some of her hurtful past to get through to the kid. "Well, whatever you said left an impression."

"Angie has work to do, but I think she's on her way."

"What was she talking about with the clothes?" He cocked his head.

"I told her I'd help her pick out some new outfits. She wants to be accepted and fit in like anyone her age. It's a good start."

Zach's chest warmed. Crystal selflessly wanted to help someone. How could he have ever thought she was shallow?

He leaned over and kissed her. "You are an amazing, giving person."

She undid her seatbelt and kissed him back, before resting her head on his shoulder. "About last night..."

"Yeah?" He stroked her hair.

"It was incredible. Can we do it again?" She gazed up at him, her eyes shining and that shy smile on her face again.

His cock sprang to life, and he had to remind himself they were on the side of a road, not in his home. Still, he wouldn't deny he wanted her again. "Yes, but not tonight. You've got to be exhausted."

She sighed and nodded. "Yeah, I am."

"I'll take a raincheck for sure." He traced a finger down her cheek, and his heart did a slow roll.

She squeezed his arm and nodded.

"It's getting late. We better head back." He kissed her again and started up the truck.

Much as he didn't want to upset her, they really needed to talk about the contract. He glanced at her, but her eyes were shut and her breathing steady. That was fast. She must have been wiped out.

Damn.

Nothing she could do about it overnight anyway, and she needed her rest. He'd find a way to talk to her in the morning.

Chapter Thirty-One

Crystal yawned and blinked her eyes. She'd slept like the dead after the stressful night. Zach had dropped her at her tent, despite Sydney's earlier threats. Maybe nothing would come of it since he hadn't interrupted any scenes.

Murphy's happy bark came from nearby, and Crystal smiled. Thank goodness he'd recovered. She dressed and stepped outside. Angie, wearing a yellow T-shirt with the park name on the front, waved and walked over with Murphy. Gone was the heavy makeup. Her face looked fresh and clean. What a difference. Best not to say anything and embarrass her.

She stopped in front of Crystal, and Murphy wagged his tail.

"He's doing better." Angie stroked the top of his head.

Crystal bent and scratched behind his ears. "Hey, guy. You gave us a scare."

Sydney's car drove down the path. She parked, got out, and approached.

Uh oh. Hopefully her coming had nothing to do with Zach. Crystal straightened.

"Good news. We're done," Sydney said.

Crystal cocked her head. "We are? It doesn't seem like you have enough material for the show."

"After last night we do. We watched the still-camera footage, and it's good stuff. Just what we needed."

Angie gasped, her eyes widening. "Wait, you mean you filmed me when Murphy got bit, and you're going to put that on TV?"

"Yup. Your parents signed a waiver for the whole family, giving us permission to use whatever we captured on camera. It was part of the deal for camping on location."

"But...but...I didn't know about that, and I had to look horrible. I was a mess. You can't show that. Everyone will make fun of me." Angie grabbed Crystal's arm. "I'll never live it down. I'm already not popular. This will ruin my life. Can't you do something?"

Crystal's blood heated. Like hell she'd let them embarrass the girl. "Don't worry, I'm not going to approve any scenes from last night. We'll have to film others."

"I'm afraid not. It says right in your contract the production company has complete control over what footage we use." Sydney held her hands up. "Guess you never read it."

Crystal's brain froze, and she shook her head. "That can't be true. My agent would have said something."

"Take it up with her. I'm just saying, we're done. I've already booked our flights back."

The hair on Crystal's arms stood at attention and every nerve fired. This couldn't be happening. All those humiliating incidents she thought they'd have to cut would air? And poor Angie was trying to change and make new friends. This would be a social media nightmare for her. Crystal had to stop them. "You can't show those scenes I wanted cut. I'm going to call my agent and get it all straightened out."

Angie's grip tightened on Crystal's arm. Murphy whined and leaned against the girl, nudging her leg with his nose.

"There's nothing you can do. The contract went through legal review and is final," Sydney said.

Cold dread sucked the air out of Crystal's lungs. "Forget about how this affects me for a second. You can't do this to Angie. Don't you have any feelings?"

Sydney shrugged. "You've been in the business long enough to know how it works. It's all about ratings and money. Nothing personal. I'll be in touch about the travel arrangements."

Crystal fumed as Sydney headed back to the car. There had to be something she could do.

Angie sniffed, and tears rolled down her cheeks.

Shit.

Crystal knew what it felt like to be splashed all over the TV as a kid and teenager.

"Why don't you go talk to your parents? They need to know about this and might have some recourse. I've got some important calls to make." Crystal squeezed her arm.

"If they put this on TV, it's the end of me. The mean girls will blast pictures on every social media platform, and the whole school will mock me."

The agony and distress in the girl's eyes clutched at Crystal's throat like a stranglehold. She'd messed up big time, and Angie was right. The other kids would rip her to shreds. "I'm sorry. I'll do everything I can to stop them."

Angie nodded and tugged Murphy's leash. "Let's go, boy."

Crystal's heart bled as they trudged up the hill, Angie swiping at her eyes.

Hoping for some help, Crystal called her agent. That ended up being a waste of time. Crystal flopped onto her sleeping bag, and pressed her eyes shut.

The conversation hadn't gone well. She had told her agent to find anything, desperate for a gig. If her agent had tried to negotiate terms, the production company would have found someone else. Plenty of down-on-their-luck celebs would have jumped at the chance. Crystal was supposed to have read through the contract and asked any questions before signing. The old Crystal had been too arrogant and aloof to bother with it. Now the new Crystal was going to suffer the consequences. And so was Angie.

A heavy weight settled in the base of her belly. She was screwed. As an influencer, she'd be a laughingstock. The companies would stop sending products, and her followers wouldn't have any faith in her endorsements after watching her dumb-ass camping antics.

If only she'd known about this earlier, she might have found a way out. With her success as an influencer and her other ideas for income, there was a chance she could have walked away and paid some minimal damages, keeping her dignity and reputation. Hell, her agent had told her there was a clause that would have allowed for limited liability if she'd ended the contract early, but the deadline had passed.

Now, it was too late. The production company owned all the footage and rights to use it.

Her phone dinged with a text from Zach.

I need to talk to you.

The weight in her gut sank deeper. Her plans to make things work if she stayed had just gone up in flames. But damn it, she loved him, even though he didn't know it. Maybe he'd have some ideas. She typed a quick reply.

I'll meet you by the lake at my camp.

She wasn't taking any chances of the still cameras filming, even though Sydney said they had enough. Crystal trudged down to the water, chastising herself with every step. She couldn't trust Sydney or anyone in Hollywood. They were all about themselves. Zach was the first person she'd ever met that she could trust, besides Jenna, and she loved him for it. Somehow, they'd figure out a way to make things work despite the dire situation.

She sat on a big rock and waited, staring at the sparkling water. This time, even the sound of the lapping ripples against the shore didn't soothe her. Taking a deep breath, she closed her eyes and tried to think of some way out of the mess.

Leaves crunched on the trail behind her, and she stood. Her stomach leapfrogged at the sight of Zach, a reaction she seemed to have on a regular basis.

"What's wrong? You look upset." He laid a hand on her

shoulder.

"Kind of everything." Her voice quivered. "I had a fight with Sydney."

"About what?"

Crystal shook her head. "The show. It's going to ruin me. She said they don't need my permission for any film they want to use, and they have a lot of really embarrassing stuff. And poor Angie, they have film of her bawling her eyes out. She's going to be devastated when it airs. It's killing me. I don't know how to stop it. I'd just earned her trust."

"I know. I'm sorry. Is there anything you can do?"

"No...I mean I could have walked away earlier, but not now." She took a breath. "Wait, what? What do you mean you know?"

He drew his hand back and rubbed his neck. "I've been trying to tell you for a while."

A shock of electricity struck her heart. He'd known about it and hadn't told her?

No. Just no...no...no...

"What are you saying? How did you know?" She held her breath, dreading the answer.

"I overheard Sydney and Trevor talking one day."

She brought a hand to her chest, unable to fathom what he'd just said. "And you didn't warn me about it? Do you know how damaging this is going to be and how it will affect Angie?"

He frowned. "Well, yeah, about you anyway, that's why I was trying to tell you."

"God, I can't believe this." Her nerves knotted into a steel ball, and her hands shook. She paced, trying to process what he'd told her. "How long have you known?"

He swallowed. "For a while. I swear I kept trying to tell you. It's why I asked you to meet me today."

"It's too late now." She held her hands up in frustration. Her head was spinning, and betrayal smashed her in the gut.

His lips pressed together in a grave line. "I told you once the producers didn't have your best interests in mind."

"You know darn well I had no clue *this* was what you meant. It's my fault for not reading the contract, but I'd mentioned many times about how I wasn't going to approve certain scenes, and you never said a word. You knew I had no idea they had the rights to use all that footage." Hot tears burned her eyes. "Did you know about this when we were up in the tree together?"

He scuffed a boot in the sand. "Yeah, but that wasn't the time to—"

"So, everything they filmed before you climbed the tree, you knew they were going to air? Me blowing that stupid whistle, the conversation about Bear. All of it and everything else from the beginning of this whole fiasco to the end?"

"I mean, I have no idea what they'll choose." He took a step toward her.

She backed up.

What bullshit. They both knew what the producers would show. To think she'd trusted him and believed she was in love with him. "Then you knew before you had sex with me, and you kept something this important a secret?" Her pulse raced, and her face turned hot.

"Yes, but we hadn't had time to talk about it yet."

She fisted a hand on her hip. "We sure talked that night, at length. It could have come up before or after sex, *certainly* before."

He opened his mouth, then shut it.

"You had to know this would destroy my influencer status and all those plans I had to make things work if I stayed here." Her voice hitched. "And you still said nothing. I must have sounded like an absolute fool. Was your family business in such dire straits that you felt like you had to string me along so the show kept filming? Never mind. Don't even answer. To think I...I...can't even."

Her chest crushed as the hope she'd had for a possible life with him crumbled. It wasn't just Hollywood people who didn't tell her the truth. Maybe no one ever would. She'd let her guard down and believed in him, thinking he was different. The real deal. Not another user.

"No. It's not like that." He shook his head.

She brushed past him, needing to get away. "Don't follow me. You're not who I thought you were. If I can't trust you, we have nothing."

When she reached her tent, she zipped herself inside and pressed her hands to her eyes. Tears leaked through her fingers. How could she have been so blind? He'd used her, just like everyone else.

A text sounded from Sydney. She'd scheduled flights for six in the morning. Of course, the cheapest travel was early, but it worked for Crystal. She'd be out of camp by three. Even Zach, the early riser, wouldn't be up and about at that time.

She checked her calendar. Crap. The rental lease on her penthouse didn't expire for three weeks. She'd have to find a place to stay. Time to phone a friend, or rather text one. Jenna would worry if she saw Crystal's tear-stained face or heard her strained voice.

She sent a text. *Done filming early. My place is rented until the end of the month. Can I crash at yours?*

Sure. The spare room is free. You have the key. If I'm not here, let yourself in. When?

Tomorrow, if that's okay?

Yup. Everything all right?

Nothing was all right, but Crystal would have a chance to talk in person later. *Yeah. Thanks a million.*

Can't wait to see you.

The ache in Crystal's heart softened. Jenna was a real friend. She was there for Crystal no matter what.

She hated to leave without saying goodbye to Erin. She'd been so kind. But she was Zach's mother, and Crystal wouldn't ever see him again. Maybe at some point she'd send Erin a note and thank her for the support.

Angie was a different story. Crystal's stomach twisted into a huge knot. What the heck could she do for that kid? An answer came to mind.

Crystal sighed, picked up her phone, and dialed Sydney's number.

Chapter Thirty-Two

Z ach rested his head against a tree, forcing himself not to follow Crystal. It took every ounce of his energy.

She was right. He'd known the show was going to air her humiliating scenes, and she had no idea. Every time he'd tried to tell her, they'd been interrupted or were dealing with something more important. As in life-threatening.

His gut had lurched when she'd asked if he'd thought to tell her before they'd had sex. They'd talked, and he'd had the opportunity. Emotion had overcome him. A rare occurrence. They'd been discussing heavy subjects before things had just...happened. It had been spontaneous and incredible. When he'd realized she was a virgin, it wasn't exactly the opportune moment to discuss the contract.

He had to respect her request for him to leave her alone. At least for tonight. She was hurting and needed time. His lungs deflated. Somehow, he'd apologize in the morning and try to explain.

He tossed and turned most of the night, staring at the ceiling. Before the sun rose, he leaped out of bed and jumped onto his UTV. Thoughts of Crystal had haunted him all night. He wouldn't wake her. He'd do his rounds and wait until she came out of her tent.

He stopped by her camping spot.

No pitched tent.

His stomach lurched. Everything had been packed and piled up, per the leaving-camp instructions. Oh, the irony. She hadn't done a single thing by the book until it was time to leave.

Leave?

She couldn't have left without telling him.

Angie stepped out of her tent with Murphy. Super early for a teenager to be awake, but maybe Murphy needed to go out. She glared at Zach. "She's gone."

"When did she leave?"

"I heard a car around three." Angie cocked her head. "Crystal was pretty hung up on you. Seems like you blew it."

"What?" He stiffened.

Angie shrugged. "I'm not blind, and tent walls are thin."

No denying it. His bruised heart banged against his ribs. Murphy trotted over and leaned against him. Zach reached down to rub behind his ears. Dogs always knew when someone was upset or in pain. He took a resigned breath. He'd hurt Crystal too much. Why else would she have fled without giving him a chance to explain and apologize?

Seeing the vacant camp dug a pit in his stomach.

Gone.

Just like that.

Zach's phone pinged with Brody's text tone.

Sydney emailed me. Heads up. They're leaving today.

Yeah, not a news flash. Zach had figured that out. He stuffed his cell back into his pocket.

Angie hung her head, and her eyes watered. "Crystal worked out a deal with the production company so they would cut me out of that snake scene. They don't need the clip of me anyway since I'm a nobody. From what I overheard, she took a big hit on the salary and got screwed by them. Crystal doesn't know that I know what she gave up. Thin walls and all."

"What?" Crystal couldn't afford to take a dock in pay. Not from what she'd told him about her finances. She was making some money as an influencer, but that was just getting started.

Angie shrugged and narrowed her eyes. "She'd been crying when she came back to her tent yesterday. And now she's gone. It's not hard to put two and two together."

Zach flinched, guilt running laps through his veins.

Angie focused on Murphy, smoothing down his fur and scratching his haunches. "You screwed up, whatever you did, but she must still care about you, because people don't cry over

someone they don't give a shit about. Just saying."

Angie tugged on Murphy's leash. "Let's go, boy."

Crystal had connected with Angie and must have gotten through to her. She acted like a different person now. Admiration swirled in his chest. She'd helped the troubled teen take a new direction. Not an easy accomplishment with the girl's former attitude.

Angie turned and called out, "Not that you deserve her. But go get her."

Chapter Thirty-Three

Z ach bagged an old AC air filter, dropped it on the floor of his
mother's house, and replaced it with a new one. As he
climbed down the ladder, her voice rang out. "I wish everything was
so easy to fix."

"What's that supposed to mean?" He glanced at her, where she
stood at the kitchen table, bundling vegetables for the co-op.

She peered at him. "Broken hearts don't mend easily. You can't
just swap one out for a fresh one."

His skin prickled. Not her too. First Angie, then his brothers
had taken him to task over Crystal leaving. They'd given him grief
for not having told her about the contract. Like he needed more
guilt. "Don't start with me, Mom."

"Why not? You've done nothing but stomp around for two
solid weeks since Crystal left. You're miserable and acting worse
than a grizzly awakened out of hibernation." She shook her head.
"When are you going to face the truth and do something about it?"

He slammed the stepladder legs together and picked up the
dirty filter. It's not like he hadn't tried. He'd called and texted her,
only to find out she'd blocked him. "There's nothing to do. Even if I
wanted to, she made her decision and told me to leave her alone."

Tsk tsk. "That's not what it sounded like the last time I spoke to her. She had plans in mind that might have worked out here. And there's only *one* reason why she would do that."

A splinter of guilt pierced his spine. He didn't need to be reminded she'd been willing to change her life for him, before he blew it. When had she discussed the future with his mom? Didn't matter. Crystal was out of his life. "I don't want to talk about her. Whatever there was between us is over."

He picked up the ladder.

His mother tossed a bunch of carrots down and crossed the room to him. "No, it's not. I won't stand by and watch you retreat into your dark hole. I can't take it a second time."

Zach blinked at the fierce pronouncement.

His mother's eyes teared. "That girl brought you back to us. I know she drove you up a wall. She also made you laugh, care, and feel. I'd almost given up hope I'd ever see the light in you again."

So had he. What the hell could he do about it now? She'd made herself clear by leaving. "Look, Mom. It's for the best. I don't have anything to offer her, and she lives a completely different lifestyle. You gotta let this go."

His mom gripped her locket necklace tightly in her hand. The one she always wore that held a wedding picture of her with his dad. "Your father taught you to fight for what you wanted. To take whatever risk it meant and to never give up. You hurt Crystal, and she lashed back. That's the way arguments go. It's time to stop licking your wounds and take action before it's too late. Time to mend fences."

Zach's breath stalled.

His mother's mouth was set in a firm line, and her fingers turned white on the locket she clutched. He'd never seen her like this. Sure, she'd reprimanded him and his brothers in the past, many times, but this was different. She had a desperate, pleading look in her eyes.

"I can't lose you again, son. I love you too much. Follow your heart." She squeezed his arm and walked away, disappearing into the kitchen.

A lump in his throat made it hard to swallow, and he stood, staring at the empty room. That comment about his father had cut deep.

Zach took the ladder outside, propped it against the house, and sat on the porch step. Was he licking his wounds? Why would he go after someone who had shut him out?

The hurt in Crystal's beautiful eyes haunted him every day, followed by the memories of her body pressed against his and the innocent, trusting way she'd shared all of herself.

From the moment he'd met her, she'd rattled his cage, showing up in her ridiculous miniskirt and heels. She drove him out of his mind with her antics, but it kept him on his toes. She was unpredictable and defiantly independent. Not to mention a smart-ass.

His chest ached at the weight that had dragged him under for the last two weeks.

God, he missed her.

The challenge, the spark, the banter, the...love.

He sat bolt upright.

The love?

Memory after memory tumbled through his mind. Crystal helping paint the spare room, walking with his mom in the gardens, listening to Zach's stories about his childhood and father. Crystal had come into his life and embraced his family. How could he have been so blind not to realize he'd fallen in love with her?

This wasn't some spoiled Hollywood fake. She was as real as they came. She'd trusted him and opened up. Made herself vulnerable. She'd been willing to change her entire life to be with him.

His heart ached as it squeezed tight.

Yes, he loved her.

What an idiot he'd been not to see it. She'd made him *feel* again. Maybe that's what he'd been fighting. If he shut everything down, it was safer. No one got hurt. But his mother was right. Living in the dark was lonely and suffocating. He'd never meant to hurt Crystal. All he'd wanted was to make her happy. Instead, he'd made her feel betrayed and had lost her trust.

Was it too late to gain it back? What if he told her he loved her? Hard to do when she'd blocked him. He didn't even know where she was anymore. Somehow, he had to find a way to reach her. If she smacked him down, at least he'd never wonder what might have been.

Chapter Thirty-Four

"Are you seriously still on the couch, wearing the same pajamas you've been living in for two weeks?" Jenna shook her head as she breezed through the family room of her flat.

"What's it matter? I'm not posting pictures of myself dressed like this." Crystal shifted and balanced her iPad on her lap. "Nothing but sunshine and happiness on my blog."

"Fake, fake, and faker. I don't know how you do it."

"It's not hard. You just pretend. Plenty of material out there to post that makes it seem like you're the happiest person in the world." Only, she was the exact opposite.

"So you're back to that? Because for a while there, you were connecting with people and posting real stuff." Jenna placed her hands on her hips.

She had a point. Crystal's followers had started to drop off. They didn't like the generic posts, and she hadn't been interacting with them as much. "It can only get worse. Once the show airs, I'll lose everyone. Who's going to be interested in anything I have to say when I look like an absolute fool?"

"It's probably not as bad as you think. Maybe you'll get more likes and follows because people appreciate someone who can laugh at themselves." Jenna frowned. "Speaking of which, you haven't smiled since you've been here. When are you going to admit you miss Zach?"

Crystal hugged a pillow to ease the empty ache inside and shook her head. "I can't trust him, so it doesn't matter what feelings I might still have for him."

Jenna pointed to Crystal. "Aha. You admit it. You *do* still love him."

"I never used the word love."

"You don't have to. I'm not blind. You haven't eaten, slept, or been yourself. You're wasting away and wallowing when you could be happy."

"I told you, I can't trust him." Crystal hugged the pillow tighter.

"Wait a minute." Jenna held up a hand. "I know you're upset he didn't tell you what was in the contract. Maybe he never had the chance. It's not like he wrote the damn thing and tricked you into signing it. There wasn't even anything in it for him."

"But—"

"No buts. I've known you your whole life and never seen you like this. You fell hard for this guy, and he apologized. He knows he screwed up. Did he ever lie to you or make you think you couldn't trust him before this happened?"

"Well...no. He doesn't play games like most guys. That's why it hurts so much. I let him in." Her heart did a slow, painful roll in her chest. The image of him staring down at her, stroking her hair after they'd made love burned in her brain.

Jenna dropped onto the couch beside her and sighed. "I've never stayed in one place long enough to fall in love with anyone. Maybe I'm the wrong one to give advice, but I don't think you're going to find another Zach. From everything you've told me, he cares about you. So he messed up. You gonna throw away a possible lifetime with him?"

"He has issues, Jenna. The war was tough on him, and he doesn't seem to need or want someone like me around. I drove him crazy the whole time I was there. We hooked up once, and now it's time to move on. Our lives are too different."

Jenna opened her mouth, then shut it and flopped back against the cushions. "Fine."

"What? You never give up." Crystal narrowed her eyes.

"First time for everything. I'm ordering a pizza, and if you don't help me eat it, I'll binge the whole thing and blame you tomorrow." Jenna patted her stomach and grinned.

"Spare me." Hiking, rock-climbing, kayaking—Jenna's job was physically demanding and kept her in top form. Crystal shrugged. "It's all yours. I don't think I can eat anything right now."

Jenna's face fell, and she shook her head. "I hate seeing you this way."

"It sucks, but soon I'll be at my penthouse again since the rental lease is almost up, and life will go on."

But would it? The thought of being back in the circuit soured her stomach. She missed the chirping of the birds and walking through the woods.

Who was she kidding? That wasn't all she missed...

Crystal opened the bedroom blinds to let in the morning sun. She tucked back a stray hair and smoothed her new skirt down. Another promotional product from a start-up company. She couldn't keep hiding from the world. If she intended to make any money, she had to get active with her blog again, and that meant advertising the products out in public.

After a quick glance in the mirror, she headed to the kitchen and poured a cup of coffee into her travel mug. Jenna had just left for work, so all was quiet. The doorbell rang, and Crystal rolled her eyes. How many times had Jenna forgotten her keys and locked herself out?

"Hold on a sec." Crystal put the lid on the cup and went to the door. She swung it open and froze at the sight of Zach, standing on the other side.

Her heart jump-started, and her mouth went dry. A million questions zipped through her brain. How did he know where to find her, and why had he come?

She blinked and shook her head. Seeing him in his familiar olive T-shirt and khaki pants made her pulse race. She tamped down the urge to fall into his arms because she was still mad at him.

He rubbed his jaw. "Can we please talk?"

Numb from shock, her brain had frozen along with her body, and she needed a second to think. "How did you know I was here?"

"Jenna called and told me."

So, that's why she'd stopped hounding Crystal about Zach. He'd traveled a long way, and he rarely left the park. Whatever caused him to fly out to see her must be important.

"Come in." She stepped aside, and he entered. Shutting the door, she took a deep breath and tried to clear her mind. "What's going on?"

He cocked his head and frowned. "First of all, are you okay? You look...tired."

No kidding. Wiped out from lack of sleep and food, sick over missing him, she'd finally pulled herself back together. But it had taken a toll. And BAM, here he was plucking at her heartstrings again.

"I'm fine." Her gaze raked up and down him. She wasn't the only person who'd lost some weight, and he had dark circles under his eyes. "You're the one who looks exhausted. Is there something wrong?"

"Yeah." He cleared his throat. "Everything."

Concern ripped through her. Was he sick? Had there been a tragedy? "What happened?"

He paced the room. "I'm sorry for not telling you what I knew about the contract. I swear it wasn't intentional."

"I'm starting to realize that."

"Wait, you are?"

"Yeah. It just hurt because I felt betrayed, and not for the first time." There, she'd said it. "People have misled and taken advantage of me my entire life, and you were the one person I trusted."

"I'm sorry." He crossed the room and stopped in front of her. "I came here to apologize in person because you won't take my calls."

She had to admit he'd gone the extra mile, and guilt gripped her. "I'm sorry for leaving without saying goodbye, but I was upset. I never meant for you to fly all the way out here to apologize. It means a lot."

He studied the floor before facing her again. "That's not the only reason I came."

"It's not?" Her pulse skittered.

"No." He reached a hand toward her face, then pulled it back. "Like I said, nothing's been the same since you left." He paced again. "I don't see things the way I used to. I miss your laugh, your antics, and the way you kept me...I don't know."

"I don't understand. I thought I drove you up the wall."

"Yeah, well, maybe I miss that too." He paused, and his Adam's apple bobbed. "I'm not used to talking about feelings, but there's something I need to say."

Her chest fluttered. Where was this going? "Okay."

"You don't see what I see in you, and you don't give yourself enough credit."

"What do you see?"

His brows knitted. "I see someone who takes on challenges when she hits rock bottom. Someone who helped a rebellious teenager turn her life around. Someone who stayed up late to paint a guest room for a woman she'd just met."

Tears blurred Crystal's vision. Somehow, being away from Hollywood had given her strength she never knew she possessed, and Zach had seen the real her.

"Oh, I almost forgot." He reached out again, and this time he stroked her cheek. "Someone who docks her own pay to protect an innocent girl from public humiliation."

Crystal raised an eyebrow, her face warming under his touch. "You know about that?"

"Yeah. That and more. It's why I…"

"What? It's why you what?"

"It's why I love you."

She blinked as her heart expanded at the words she'd never dreamed she'd hear from him. "Hold on. This is a lot to—"

"Just hear me out."

Her breath hitched, and she waited.

"I want you in my life. Yes, I love you." He lowered his head and gave her a gentle, soft kiss.

His words crashed through her, evoking a cascade of emotions. He loved her?

"There's more." He placed his hands on her shoulders with a light, tentative touch. "My family wants you in their lives too. Mom said she'd love your help with the wedding venue business, and Brody admitted we need a marketing person for the park. We'd like to hire you."

"Wait, what?" Crystal's head was spinning. This couldn't be happening. Zach had talked to his family and followed up on the plans she had mentioned? "But when this stupid reality show airs, my status might go up in flames."

"I'm not worried about it. We wouldn't be hiring you for your status. Whatever you do on your own as an influencer is above and beyond the job. I believe in you. You can overcome anything. I'm the one who has issues, and even that's better when we're together."

And just like that, she melted and the tears flowed. This man, who had seen more trauma in his life than she could ever imagine, had faith in *her*. "You are the strongest person I've ever met. You helped me when I felt most vulnerable and out of my element. You shared your family with me. That was a gift."

He brushed her tear with his thumb and wrapped his arms around her. "I can't stand to see you cry. All I ever want to do is make you smile."

She hugged him back as memories of their time together

flooded back. Her gruff Grizzly had turned out to be a strong man of character and compassion. He'd flown across the country to make an in-person apology for something that, truth be told, she should have known all along.

He kissed the top of her head, took a deep breath, and stepped back. "I know you'd be giving up a lot to leave your Hollywood life, but I wouldn't ask you to without something to offer."

"What do you mean?"

He fished in his pocket, pulled out a velvet box, and dropped to his knee.

Oh my God. He couldn't be about to...could he? Blood pounded in her head, and her legs went weak.

The slightest tremor shook his normally firm, steady hand as he opened the ring box and held it up. "I love you. I want to spend the rest of my life with you. Will you marry me?"

Sheer love for him pulsed through her body. Whatever came their way, they would handle together. Just the thought of going back with him launched her heart sky-high. Too choked up to speak, she nodded.

His eyes blazed, and a relieved grin lit up his face as he stood, slipped the ring onto her finger, and kissed her.

"I love you too," she whispered against his lips, saying the words that had been singing in her soul since she'd fallen for him, and he'd caught her.

Epilogue

Brody brought up a spreadsheet of the park's finances and color-coded the line items. He rubbed his forehead to ease the tension. For the first time in a while, the numbers looked promising. Crystal's marketing and promotions over the last three months had resulted in more bookings. He'd had a scare when the network didn't pick up *Celebrity Trials*. They'd gone with some kitchen-wars show instead. He'd have thought people were sick of those, but what did he know?

As it turned out, Crystal's influencer status remained intact, and she'd brought in business. Maybe even more than the show would have if it ran, because that was a onetime deal, but she continued to post and promote daily. People liked her, and she kept gaining followers.

He shoved back from the computer and ran a hand through his hair. Brody never would have thought Zach would fall for someone like Crystal. They were complete opposites. Yet, having her in his life had changed Zach. Not that he didn't still have his grumpy moments, but he actually smiled again. There was a lightness about him that Brody hadn't seen in years. A weight in his chest lifted. He'd missed his once carefree brother and was glad that Zach had found someone who made him happy.

Brody wasn't holding out for that to happen to him. He'd already laid his heart on the line and been burned. Nope. He'd never risk falling in love again. Been there, done that.

"Hey, Brody." Zach entered the room, headed to the coffeepot, and poured a cup. "What a shock. Levi isn't here yet."

"I heard that. I was right on your heels." Levi smirked and sauntered into the room. "Maybe if you weren't daydreaming about Crystal, you would have heard me."

"Off to a great start." Brody shook his head.

"You're just jealous," Zach said to Levi with a teasing, self-satisfied smile.

"Are you kidding me? I could have had her. I stepped back for you. You owe me." Levi bowed and waved a hand, a grin on his face. "You're welcome."

"Can you two knock it off so we can talk business?" Brody straightened. They had important things to discuss.

Levi and Zach took a seat and sipped their coffee.

He paged through his spreadsheet. "The forecast is good for the upcoming season. We need to discuss the details of this adventure program. It can bring in a whole new source of income and customers."

"I'm all for it, but we'll need to hire a guide. None of us has the time to take people on trips," Levi said.

"I already talked to Brody about that." Zach shifted in his chair. "Crystal's friend, Jenna, wants to interview for it. She has a lot of experience, and the place she works at is going out of business."

Brody's chest tightened. He didn't trust an outsider to come in and run a new part of the business. "If we decide to hire someone, I'd want it to be a local. Someone who knows us and the area. Besides, I'm not convinced we need to. Crystal is handling the marketing, and we can hire a temp to help with the administrative work. That would free up some time for me to handle the new venture."

Levi frowned. "No doubt you could do it. We all grew up rock-climbing, hiking, and kayaking. But we're talking about some overnight trips, and I don't see you having that much time. Plus, there's the planning, bookings, and meal arrangements. I think we need to hire someone."

He had a point. Adding in those tasks would eat up chunks of the day. Still, this was a family business and a brand-new venture. He wasn't ready to hand that off to someone. "Maybe we start small and just do a few day trips."

"I don't think that will bring in much business." Zach shook his head. "Jenna told Crystal that they take busloads of people and have multiple guides on tours, unless it's some remote place in another country. But we'll be staying within a few hours of the park. There's money in numbers."

"I don't like it. We'd be putting a lot of responsibility in the hands of whoever we hired, and the park's reputation is on the line," Brody said.

"That's why we hire someone who knows what they're doing." Zach rubbed his chin. "Jenna's been at this for a long time, and she's been all over the world. With her experience, I'm sure she'd be more than capable of running the show."

The last thing Brody wanted was some know-it-all taking over the operation. "Well, she's never been here. She has no idea how things work for us."

Levi held up his hands. "There's no point in doing something half-assed. Either we go all out and hire someone, or we forget about it. I know you're a control freak, Brody, but you gotta let go sometime."

Brody bristled, his blood heating. "Just because I'm not willing to take risks with outsiders doesn't make me a control freak. It's—"

"Everyone simmer down. Let's stick to the topic." Zach tapped his fingers on the armrest. "Do we all agree that we'd make money and grow the business if we added the program?"

"Yes," Levi said.

Brody hesitated, not liking where Zach was going. But Brody couldn't argue the fact. He gave a quick nod.

"Then it's time for a vote." The corners of Zach's mouth curved up. "I say we post the job listing."

And there it was. Payback for when they'd outvoted Zach on the decision to let *Celebrity Trials* film there. Only that had turned out well for Zach, who never would have met Crystal otherwise.

"I agree." Levi gave a thumbs up.

Brody's stomach sank. Easy for them to vote yes. They wouldn't have to deal with the new person. Delegating wasn't Brody's strong suit. He'd learned the hard way that if you wanted a job done right, you did it yourself. "I guess it doesn't matter what I say then."

"Lighten up, Brody. It's gonna work out for the best. One question, Zach." Levi faced him. "Is Jenna hot?"

Zach cleared this throat. "Since I'm engaged, I don't look at other woman anymore. But if I did—"

"That's it. This meeting is over." Brody stood.

Levi snickered as he and Zach set their cups on the counter.

Wonderful. They'd bonded since Zach's newfound love had come along, and he wasn't such a grump.

"This is going to be great for the business. Wait and see," Zach said.

Brody's insides twisted.

Yeah, right.

Thank you for reading! Did you enjoy? Please add your review because nothing helps an author more and encourages readers to take a chance on a book than a review.

And don't miss more from Diane Holiday with <u>LOVE IN HIDING</u>, available now. Turn the page for a sneak peek!

You can also sign up for the City Owl Press newsletter to receive notice of all book releases!

Sneak Peek of Love in Hiding

If she hoped to live, Sarah Cooper needed to pull off the most convincing performance of her life.

A disappearing act.

The GPS's robo-voice announced she'd arrived at her destination. A white wooden sign that read *Oak Ridge Farms* with a bucking black stallion marked the entrance. She glanced in the rearview mirror one last time to make sure no one had followed her. Tension eased from her stiff neck. She'd white-knuckled the drive on the freeway out of San Diego almost a week ago. At least the quiet country lanes in rural Maryland had prevented anyone from sneaking up on her.

She turned onto a tree-lined, dirt driveway, and her heart rate kicked up a notch.

This ranch was her last hope and the only job left that included room and board. No more sleeping cramped in her car.

She eyed the low-fuel light. The gas tank was as empty as her stomach. Nerves jitterbugged up her spine. She knew nothing about horses or farms. From the time she could walk, her life had been dance, dance, dance. Her slim build, perfect for ballet, wasn't an asset when interviewing for jobs requiring manual labor. None of the other jobs had panned out. She clenched her molars.

This interview would be different. It had to be.

Rocks and dirt crunched under the tires of the dinged-up Honda she'd bought. At some point, she'd owe a boatload of money to a parking garage in California where she'd abandoned her almost-new Toyota.

It didn't matter. A dead woman had no use for a nice car.

She pulled up to a maroon and white-trimmed barn. In the distance, a sprawling, tan house sat atop a grassy hill. Horses grazed in spacious fields enclosed by brown, split-rail fences between the stables and woods. Open meadows stretched for miles.

Peace and freedom. What she wouldn't give to have those again.

She took a deep breath, snatched the help-wanted ad from the seat beside her, and stepped out to find the owner. On her way toward the stables, she zipped her baggy jacket. Early May weather didn't call for a coat, but with luck, her slight frame would look bigger, and Debbie wouldn't worry about hiring someone too small to do the work.

A gust of wind blew the newspaper clipping out of her hand. The scrap skittered along the dirt, and she lunged to grab it. Her fingers touched the edge but another gust set the paper back in flight. She scrambled, rounding the corner of the barn, and smacked headfirst into a pair of booted legs. The impact threw her back, and she landed on her butt. Her fight-or-flight instinct kicked in before logic, and she tensed.

Her gaze climbed and climbed before reaching a man's face shadowed by the brim of a navy ball cap with a Wounded Warrior emblem. Electric blue eyes stared down at her with such intensity her breath caught.

"Are you okay?" He offered a hand.

God no, but she couldn't tell him that. "Yes."

Her first lie of the day.

One flex of his strong forearm and she found herself on her feet again. She'd never had one of her dance partners lift her up with such ease. Or grace. But something told her if she called this guy graceful, he wouldn't take it as a compliment.

He stepped back and crossed his arms. "Can I help you?"

She glanced up at his still-shadowed face, from his chiseled chin to the jagged scar at the edge of his right cheekbone. Thick, corded muscles lined his neck, and broad shoulders stretched his camouflage T-shirt. No doubt, physical work shaped his body, not a weight room.

His guarded eyes seemed to see right through her.

She forced herself not to squirm.

The breeze blew the clean fragrance of soap and leather toward her. She inhaled the pure, masculine scent, getting a little lightheaded.

He cleared his throat.

She jumped and mentally slapped herself, kicking her libido to the backseat. With her life in danger, she needed to stay focused.

"I'm looking for Debbie. I called about the ad in the paper, and she told me to come out." Sarah squared her shoulders and ignored the warmth rising to her cheeks.

He hitched an eyebrow. "You're here to apply for the farmhand job?"

"Yes." She nodded. Best to keep the conversation short. The doubt on his face only meant more questions and possible trouble. "Can you tell me where I might find Debbie?"

"She's probably at the house for lunch." He waved up the hill at a large rancher with a white wraparound porch. "And you are?"

"Sarah." At least she'd kept her first name the same. Less chance of slipping up.

He held out his hand. "Bruce."

When her palm pressed against his calloused one, a ripple of awareness passed through her.

Wheels crunched on the gravel behind them. She whipped her head around and froze, straining to make out the person behind the wheel. A woman emerged from the car, and Sarah heaved a big sigh.

A frown tugged at the corner of Bruce's mouth. "That's some grip you have."

She jerked her hand away and bit her cheek. Not five minutes on the premises and she'd panicked. She couldn't blow this chance. The small horse farm, located on the opposite coast from California, would make her hard to find. Sure, she'd have to learn about horses, but the job didn't call for any experience.

"Should I wait here for Debbie to come back?"

He adjusted his cap. "I was just headed up. I'll take you to find her."

"Thanks. I appreciate that." Although, she'd rather not spend any more time with the man.

She turned to follow him and stepped into a rut. He whipped an arm out and steadied her before she fell. Damn. Another wave of heat burned a path to her face. She'd have to watch her footing and calm her nerves around this guy or he'd think her a total klutz. The furthest thing from the truth.

He drew his hand back and glanced at her mud-caked tennis shoes but said nothing. She'd need boots if she got the job, which might be a stretch given her rocky start.

"Why do you want to work here? You don't look like a typical farmhand," Bruce asked as they trekked across the field.

"I need a job, and this one includes room and board. My lease is up." Only a half lie because she did need the work. She'd better change the subject. "Do you keep a horse here?"

He nodded. "Yes. But I also run a therapy program at the farm."

Sweat trickled down the side of her neck. She glanced over her shoulder. Every step farther from her car tightened the knot in her stomach. At least she had her gun in her purse. Not that she'd learned to shoot it yet.

Bruce climbed the steps leading to the porch. A couple of wooden rockers and a wicker table with two chairs sat under the shade of the roof. An orange tabby cat, rolled into a lazy ball, slept in the far corner.

"Deb, you there?" Bruce called through the screen door.

"Come on in," yelled a woman with a gruff, husky voice. "I got plenty of soup. You hungry?"

He shot a glance at Sarah and opened the door, holding it wide for her. "No, thanks."

Sarah entered the house. The scent of biscuits wafted through the room, and her stomach grumbled. She hadn't eaten since last night. Her body ran on nothing but adrenaline now.

Sun streamed through a bay window in the airy, open kitchen. Hanging plants dangled over clay containers of fresh herbs on the ledge. A large pot simmered on the stove. Homey. She missed the feeling. Homey had ended for her at age fourteen when she'd left for the dance academy in New York.

Her gaze went to the windows. Neither the bay one nor the two over the sink had curtains. Anyone could see right in. She pressed a hand to her throat.

A woman with short brown hair, wearing jeans and a red flannel shirt, stood by the stove stirring soup. She glanced over her shoulder at them and placed a lid on the pot. Probably in her mid-fifties, though hard to tell with her deeply tanned skin, she had several inches and a good thirty pounds on Sarah.

"This is Sarah. She wants to apply for the job you listed," Bruce said.

Sarah stood as tall as possible while Debbie looked her up and down.

"You a friend of Bruce's?" Debbie crossed the room to them.

"No. I kinda bumped into him." At least the first words out of her mouth to Debbie weren't a lie.

Debbie scratched her head, as if she didn't know what to make of Sarah, and faced Bruce. "Since when do you turn down my chicken soup?"

Bruce's gaze darted from Sarah to the door. "No time. I have to get the horse ready for Charlie."

Debbie checked her watch and frowned. "But it's only—"

"Gotta go."

He left without a backward glance and let the screen door slam behind him.

Sarah blinked at his abrupt departure. His relationship with Debbie must be solid for him to feel free to act so rudely.

Bruce hiked away from the house at a brisk clip, not sure what to make of Sarah. The tiny woman wearing a jacket two sizes too big didn't belong doing a job that required hard physical labor.

No mistaking that look of fright on her face earlier. He'd seen it enough to last a lifetime. He set his jaw and scanned the perimeter. Tall grass swayed in the empty fields, and the surrounding woods were quiet. Nothing out of place. Yet something or someone had this woman spooked.

Despite her small frame, she carried herself in a way that made her seem taller, and he hadn't missed the spark in her eyes when he'd questioned her about working at the farm. But the dark half-moons under them and the tightness in her face were textbook signs of stress and lack of sleep.

With large emerald eyes, fair skin, and wavy, dark hair, her striking features could turn any man's head. Yet, something had stirred inside him when her cheeks turned pink.

He tamped it down.

Didn't want it.

Didn't need it.

Most of the women he'd worked with in the Navy were tough from the job and didn't blush. Not much different at the farm, for that matter. Sarah had a softness about her, a vulnerability, but also spunk to think she could hold her own.

He frowned and continued on his way.

"Whoa."

Someone tapped his elbow, and he swung around to find himself face to face with his uncle Joe.

Crap.

Of all people.

"Where's the fire?" Wrinkles formed on the sides of his brown eyes as he squinted against the sun.

A vein pulsed in Bruce's temple. He never flew under Joe's radar. All the years Bruce had spent in the Navy, no one could read him. It's what had made him one of their best operatives. But Joe?

It was like he was hardwired to Bruce's brain. The man didn't miss a damn thing.

"I'm headed to the stables." Bruce glanced at Joe's hand still on his arm.

Joe let go but didn't move to leave. "Why do you look like you saw a ghost?"

Bruce would rather break in new boots with a blister than discuss his feelings. Yeah, he had a ghost, and he wasn't about to betray her. "Everyone's full of questions today. I'll never get to the barn at this rate."

"Uh-huh." Joe's eyes narrowed. "I just left there. The place is still standing."

"Well, I have stuff to do before Charlie shows up." He needed to get away before Joe dug any deeper. Turning his back, Bruce called over his shoulder, "See you later."

He strode toward the barn. When he entered, the sweet scent of hay filled his nostrils. Horses snorted in their cool, dark stalls. He worked his way down the aisle, stopping to stroke their heads as they poked them over the half doors.

As usual, when he came to Misty's stall, the old mare neighed and nudged his hand. His heart squeezed. She might not be around much longer. The last of his father's horses, and what a trooper. Misty had turned out to be a perfect therapy horse. She'd been gentle and sweet from day one. His father had chosen well when he'd bought her for Bruce's early lessons. Maybe his dad would have been proud of what Bruce had done with Misty and the program. He needed to stay focused. The veterans depended on him.

He pulled a sugar cube out of his pocket and held out his open palm. Her warm, fat lips swiped the treat away to crunch.

Through his work, he'd found a way to cope with the losses in his life. He didn't need complications like Sarah stirring up unwanted feelings.

Debbie wouldn't hire her. Hell, the twelve-year-olds who helped after school in exchange for riding time were bigger. She'd have to find someplace else to work. They didn't need whatever trouble might follow her to the ranch. This farm, his patients, and the people he worked with were his family. He'd protect them at all costs.

Any minute now, Sarah would get back in her car and leave.

A kitten Debbie had taken in rubbed against his leg, and a knot formed in the pit of his stomach.

Shit.

Debbie had a soft spot for strays. He'd have to make sure Sarah wasn't her next one.

Don't stop now. Keep reading with your copy of <u>LOVE IN HIDING</u>.

And sign up for Diane's newsletter to get all the news, giveaways, excerpts, and more!

Don't miss more from Diane Holiday with LOVE IN HIDING, available now, and discover all her books at www.dianeholiday.com

Running from danger, caught by love.

With her life at risk, Sarah Cooper hangs up her ballet shoes and flees her glamorous career in San Diego. She assumes a new identity and takes refuge at a horse ranch in rural Maryland. Mucking stalls is a far cry from center stage, and the ranch's so-called "horse whisperer" is the complete opposite of the men she's used to. He's stubborn, sullen, and sexy.

Unfortunately, he's also suspicious. Of her.

Bruce Murphy trusts his horses, and since the new ranch hand showed up, they've been skittish. Sarah's trouble, and Bruce wants her gone before he loses anyone else he cares about. She challenges him until he can't decide if he should kiss or shake her. But the more time they spend together, the more he sees the truth: Sarah isn't trouble, she's in trouble.

Bruce protects his heart as tightly as Sarah guards her secrets, but they each have something the other needs—Sarah needs Bruce to help her stay alive and Bruce needs Sarah to help him learn to live again.

Please sign up for the City Owl Press newsletter for chances to win special subscriber-only contests and giveaways as well as receiving information on upcoming releases and special excerpts.

All reviews are **welcome** and **appreciated**. Please consider leaving one on your favorite social media and book buying sites.

Escape Your World. Get Lost in Ours! City Owl Press at www.cityowlpress.com.

Acknowledgments

I'd like to express my sincere thanks to all who have supported me in my writing career:

To my family, Steve, Kelsey, and Brent, who are my biggest fans and always there to cheer me on.

To my talented critique partners, Renee, Miguella, Karen and Steve. Your inputs are invaluable to me.

To City Owl Press co-founders Tina Moss, Yelena Casale, and editor, Mary Cain.

To my loyal readers and neighbors, who good-naturedly hound me for the next release.

To anyone who devotes their time to helping animals in any capacity.

To all who serve or have served in the military. Your sacrifices are greatly appreciated.

I feel blessed to have these people in my life and for the gift of being able to create the stories that swirl around in my head.

About the Author

DIANE HOLIDAY is an award-winning author who writes romantic suspense and contemporary romance with a healthy dose of humor. Her characters will make you laugh, cry, and root for them to the end. If you are sleep deprived because you couldn't put her book down, then she's achieved her goal.

She and her husband, a retired Navy Captain, who is her go-to for colorful slang and guy-talk, live in South Carolina on beautiful Lake Murray. Diane loves dogs and features one in each of her books. In her spare time, she volunteers at a rescue farm for large-breed dogs and another no-kill shelter national organization.

www.dianeholiday.com

 facebook.com/DianeHolidayBooks

 instagram.com/diholiday333

About the Publisher

City Owl Press is a cutting edge indie publishing company, bringing the world of romance and speculative fiction to discerning readers.

Escape Your World. Get Lost in Ours!

www.cityowlpress.com

f facebook.com/CityOwlPress

X x.com/cityowlpress

⊙ instagram.com/cityowlbooks

ⓟ pinterest.com/cityowlpress

♪ tiktok.com/@cityowlpress